SORRY,

BESTIE

FELICITY T. ABBOTT

ILLUSTRATIONS BY
KAREN GARDINER ARMSTRONG

Blessings
Felicity T. Abbott

WESTBOW
PRESS®
A DIVISION OF THOMAS NELSON
& ZONDERVAN

This is a work of fiction. All of the characters, names, incidents, organizations, and dialogue in this novel are either the products of the author's imagination or are used fictitiously.

WestBow Press books may be ordered through booksellers or by contacting:

WestBow Press
A Division of Thomas Nelson & Zondervan
1663 Liberty Drive
Bloomington, IN 47403
www.westbowpress.com
844-714-3454

Illustrations by Karen Gardiner Armstrong

Scripture taken from the New King James Version® Copyright © 1982 by Thomas Nelson. Used by permission. All rights reserved.

ISBN: 978-1-6642-1252-7 (sc)
ISBN: 978-1-6642-1251-0 (hc)
ISBN: 978-1-6642-1253-4 (e)

Library of Congress Control Number: 2020922675

Print information available on the last page.

WestBow Press rev. date: 12/07/2020

Bam! Bam! Bam! At six in the morning, the alarm clock sounded like a jackhammer in my head.

"Happy birthday to you! Happy birthday to you! Happy birthday, dear Lacy! Happy birthday to you! Time to get up and get ready for school. You don't want to be late, especially on the first day."

Thanks, Mom, I thought. *Just what I wanted—to be reminded that I have to go to school on my birthday.*

Couldn't school have waited just one more day? One more day to rest peacefully on my fluffy pillows that felt like soft, wispy clouds. One more day to stay in bed as long as I wanted. One more day to hang around in my pajamas until I felt like pulling on my bathing suit to cool off in the lake. One more day. Just one more day! Was it really that much to ask?

"Rise and shine and give God the glory, glory. Rise and shine, children of the Lord."

Oh, no. My mom was singing at me again as she came in and raised the blinds, letting the sunlight stream into my room.

"Come on, Lacy. You can't stay in bed any longer. Get up and get ready for school. We want to start the year off right."

How can she be so cheery in the morning? How can anyone be happy in the morning? I just wanted to bury my head under the pillows and scream at the top of my lungs. I was not looking forward to the rest of the day.

I lay there thinking about last year. Last year, I had friends. Last year, Grace, Marie, and Jade were all there. Grace and Marie were new to the school, but Jade wasn't. She was my best friend. In fact, we had been best friends since we were four years old. We always had so much fun together, making jewelry or swimming or, you know, just hanging out. I could always rely on Jade. We would sit together at lunch, race for the swings at break, and sing. We sang all the time. Oh, the good old days!

"Your breakfast is ready!" Mom yelled from the kitchen.

Oh no! Is it already six thirty? I thought as I hurried to the bathroom to shower.

"No time for breakfast!" I yelled as I shut the door to the bathroom.

"It's seven thirty!" Mom shouted. "Your lunch is packed. I'll start the car. Let's go!"

I grabbed my sweater and ran down the stairs to the kitchen. There was Sticky, our toy poodle, looking up at me.

"Oh, Sticky, you're just so fluffy! Give me a hug!" Like a bolt of lightning, she streaked past me and out of my reach. I chased her around the table until I heard the beeping. "You win this time, but I will get a hug when I get home," I vowed.

Sticky, quite pleased with herself, sat panting under the table with what I supposed was a smirk on her face.

Mom was glaring at me as I got in the car. "Lacy, you really have to be faster in the morning. You're in high school now. You're not a baby anymore. You have to be more responsible."

I nodded in agreement but felt that she didn't understand. I had to shower, brush my teeth, fix my hair, and put on that awful acne cream.

"Did you remember everything you need for today? This is a gym day. You do have your gym uniform, right?"

"What? You're not serious! Gym on the first day of school? Of course I don't have it!" I whined. This was not going to be a terrific birthday.

We pulled into the school parking lot at 7:57 a.m. I had three minutes to grab my stuff, throw it all into my locker, and run to homeroom.

As I opened the main door, I noticed that the hallways were already empty. Panicked, I ran as fast as I could to my locker, put my jacket away, turned around, and bumped right into Kyle—sweet, sensitive Kyle. I'd only been crushing on him for two years.

He looked down at me, his bright blue eyes sparkling. "Oh, I didn't see you there. Are you okay?"

"F-f-f-f-ine," I stammered and hurried to homeroom, sure that my face was as red as my uniform shirt, which must have looked fantastic with the explosion of zits I saw on my forehead that morning.

I slid into my seat at exactly eight, just as Pastor Dave began the announcements over the intercom.

"Good morning and welcome, students and staff," he said. "We are all looking forward to a great year filled with opportunities to learn. Every day is a gift from God, given to us to reach for our potential. Please use each day to learn and grow and to learn and grow in the Lord. Please remember the following events. This afternoon is tryouts for the girls' volleyball team and boys' soccer team. Ladies in middle and high school are encouraged to be at the gym right after school. Boys will meet on the field directly after school."

I cringed inwardly while Pastor Dave gave the morning announcements. All the girls in my class would be trying out for the volleyball team. It was practically expected that we would all play and want to be on the team. Personally, I hated sports. Why in the world would people want a ball hurtling toward their face? I might not have been a supermodel, but I wanted to keep my face intact! I was lucky to make it through gym class. Why would I voluntarily sign up for torture? The bell rang, and everyone started toward their first class.

I had heard rumors over the summer that there would be a new kid in our class—a boy. I had been so excited. Someone new! There had been new kids the past two years, but they had been girls, and besides, they didn't stay at the school. Having a boy in class would be great!

There weren't any boys in class last year, and there had only been two boys the years before that. Jake and Michael had made class interesting, always asking funny questions. Unfortunately for Michael, Jake preferred to hang out with the girls, so Michael had to make friends with the boys in seventh grade.

Yup, Jake definitely liked the girls. At the beginning of the year, he had a crush on Alyssa. Then he was always with Amanda. By Christmas, he was pulling Kate's braids and teasing her, and finally in June, Jake was hanging with Rachel. I never did understand why he was always with them. I mean, I guess they're pretty, but they're so mean, and all they do is complain. Anyway, Jake and Michael both left for other schools, so there was only Alyssa's group and us: Jade, Marie, Grace, and me.

I got to my first class and looked around. No boy. Of course Alyssa and Rachel were there, laughing as I walked in. Amanda, Kate, Aimee, and Laura were already in their seats. No boy in sight! I was so disappointed. I truly would be stuck with just them.

"Good morning, ladies. Nice to see you back," said Mrs. Hart cheerily. "As you know, this is ninth-grade English. I'll get you your books in a moment, but since we all already know one another, let's start by sharing a little bit of our summer vacations. What did everyone do?"

Rachel was the first to answer. "Oh, it was great! Alyssa has a beach house. I slept over, and we had an awesome time!"

"Yeah," said Kate. "I was there last week, and it was the best!"

"Me too," chimed in Rachel and Aimee.

Rachel added, "It was so much fun riding the waves."

Then Laura said, "Yeah, her beach house rocked!" Then she showed off her tan.

Mrs. Hart smiled and said, "Sounds like you all had fun. What about you, Amanda?"

Amanda pretended to pout. "My tan is gone! I visited Alyssa at the beginning of the month. Then we had to leave to drive my brother to college."

"Lacy, you haven't said anything yet. What did you do all summer?" Mrs. Hart asked sweetly.

Suddenly, all eyes were on me. I wanted to run away. I hadn't done anything exciting. Besides, I didn't even know that Alyssa had gone to the beach, never mind had a beach house! I was so embarrassed and humiliated. Everyone else had been invited; why wasn't I? I'd gone to school with Alyssa since kindergarten. It wasn't fair!

"We drove my sister to college too," I answered in a hoarse whisper, my eyes fighting back tears.

Mrs. Hart moved closer. "I'm sorry. Could you repeat what you said, Lacy? No one could hear you."

"We drove to South Carolina to take Dakota to college," I said as I wiped away a tear, hoping that no one noticed.

"Oh," replied Mrs. Hart, the smile fading from her face.

"Well, we have a lot to do, so I'll pass out your books now," said Mrs. Hart as she moved to the bookshelf.

"Oh?" All she had said was "Oh?" I suppose I should have been grateful that she even remembered I was there. After all, no one else had.

Finally, the bell rang, and we moved to the next class—history with Mrs. White.

"This year," she announced, "you will be doing a lot of projects. We will be studying the American colonies first, so your first project will be to create a map of the colonies that does the following: (1) gives its geographic location; (2) shows what natural resources were available; and (3) indicates whether the colonists there were Tories or Revolutionaries. Pick a partner to work with, and I'll hand out the rubric and your books. Then we can get started with chapter 1."

Pick a partner. She had said it so casually, but my heart started thumping wildly as I frantically looked around the room for a friend. A friend... Who was I kidding? I had no friends! Marie hadn't come back that year, and Jade had left too. My best friend had ditched me! I was alone. I had no one.

I glanced around the room. Of course Alyssa and Rachel had paired up. Kate was moving toward Amanda. Laura waved to Aimee to come over. I sat there by myself.

Mrs. White started passing out the books. "Oh," she said, "there's seven of you. That's okay. There can be a group of three."

All the girls turned to stare at me. Alyssa was laughing as usual. Rachel had a look on her face that said, "No way are you working with us."

Kate and Amanda looked away and started chatting.

"Lacy can work with you girls, right, Laura?" said Mrs. White helpfully.

"Uh-huh," replied Laura as she looked over at Aimee, rolling her eyes.

"No, it's okay," I said quietly. "I can do it by myself."

"Well, it's really supposed to be a team effort," responded Mrs. White, "but since there is an uneven number in the class, it will be fine this time. However, you all will have to choose a different partner for each project as the year progresses."

I breathed a sigh of relief. I could do the project myself.

Science class was next with Mrs. Strickland. I liked Mrs. Strickland. She was our homeroom, science, and Bible teacher the year before. She tried to make science fun by having us do experiments in class. The best ones were when she brought in food. Also, she brought us on cool field trips. My favorite was the llama farm. I hoped science would be like last year. Sure enough, Mrs. Strickland had a list of possible field trips written on the board.

"Ooh!" I squealed. "A whale watch!"

"Why would we want to do that?" said Rachel, who acted like she was too cool for something so boring.

"Yeah," said Amanda. "You'd probably get seasick!"

Everybody giggled.

Mrs. Strickland just shook her head and said, "These are some of the trips we might go on. Since this is a small class, we'll be able to do a lot. Please give me any ideas you have for a trip."

Then she handed us a packet. As soon as I looked at it, I groaned inwardly. At the very top of the first page, in big bold letters, were the words Science Fair Project.

Then I heard Mrs. Strickland trying to reassure us. "No worries. The science fair is in March. We have all year to work on this, and I will go through it with you step by step. The main thing will be that you understand the scientific method."

Alyssa raised her hand. "Mrs. Strickland," she said sweetly, "can we work with a partner?"

No! I thought. *No! No! No! Say No!* I prayed, *Please, God, let her say no partners.*

Mrs. Strickland looked up from her desk. "I haven't decided yet. I'll think about it."

Alyssa smiled at Rachel, who smiled and nodded back at her.

Lunchtime! I couldn't believe how hungry I was. I hurried to my locker to get my lunch bag and then headed into the cafeteria/gym. All the high schoolers had lunch at the same time. The rule was you sat with your grade to eat lunch. Then you were allowed to play ball or hang out with whomever you wanted until the bell rang.

I sat at one of the ninth-grade tables as everyone made their way in with their friends.

Kate and Amanda sat at the table in front of the one I was sitting at.

The tenth graders came in and sat at the table behind me.

Then I heard the eleventh graders laughing and joking and turned to see Brett clowning around as usual. He was pretending to be so thirsty that he was dying. Everyone was laughing as he crawled over to the water fountain, yelling "Agua! I need *agua*!" Oh, Brett!

Alyssa and Rachel bought some chips and went to sit with Kate and Amanda.

Laura and Aimee sauntered in from the restroom with their hair freshly brushed and plunked themselves down with the rest of the group of ninth-grade girls.

I watched from my table as they chatted and took turns braiding each other's hair. I slowly ate my lunch, and even though I was hungry, I didn't touch the fruit or the cookies my mom had packed. I couldn't. My stomach was in knots. If this was the year before, I would have been sitting with Marie and Jade. I always sat next to Jade. I remember once when Marie and I argued over it. I had to sit next to Jade. No one else could. After all, she was *my* best friend. I wondered who she was sitting with now.

I got up to use the restroom. On the way there, I had to pass the teachers' lunch table. That's when I heard it: "Poor Lacy. She's not herself today. She started to cry in class when she told us about Dakota leaving for college."

"The poor dear," agreed Mrs. Strickland. "She must miss her sister. They have a close relationship."

I didn't want to hear anymore. I edged my way to the restroom through a blur a tears, getting there just in time before I threw up.

Note to Jade

Hi, Jade!

Just sitting here in study hall. I don't have any real homework yet, so I have time to write you a note.

You know how we heard that there was going to be a new boy here this year? Well, it turns out that he's in tenth grade, not ninth.

I pretty much have all the same teachers as last year. Mrs. Strickland is still teaching science, but Mrs. Hart and Mrs. White have switched. Mrs. Hart is teaching English this year, and Mrs. White is teaching history.

Do you have pre-algebra? I was supposed to, but things got changed, and it isn't being offered. We all have just plain old math with Mr. Grimes.

Oh yeah, Mrs. Strickland is teaching Bible too.

There is a choice of a cooking or a sewing class. If you were here, I know we'd have a blast sewing outfits for our dolls. I don't know. I'll probably choose cooking. Sewing won't be much fun without you.

We also will have French class three times a week with Madame Rêve. (When she wrote her name on the board, she put that funny little hat over the e. She said it was some type of accent mark.) Do you remember how much we wanted French class? Oh, how I wish you were here!

Not much has changed here. All the same girls are in the class, except you and Marie.

Alyssa had a beach house over the summer. It seems like everybody from class was invited. Did you go?

Mrs. Strickland put a list of field trips on the board. The most interesting one is a whale watch. You would love that! Remember when we went to the llama farm and Brett chased the llamas until he slipped and fell in the poop? LOL!

Oh, you know how I like Kyle, right? I almost ran right into him, *literally*. He's still as cute as ever!

Well, I gotta go. I hope we can get together soon. Maybe you can come over this weekend?

Your twin and bestie,
Lacy

"Hi, honey! I hope you had a great day!" Mom said, smiling as she swung the car door open for me to get in.

"Uh huh," I answered.

"How were your classes? Did you meet the new student?" she asked with a lilt in her voice.

Silence.

She tried again. "How many kids are in your class? Were the teachers nice?"

Again, I didn't answer. I simply did not want to talk about it, any of it, especially to Mom.

She really wanted me to be happy and to love school. She and Dad chose this school so I could have nice Christian friends and get a good education. They thought a small school was better because there would be fewer "distractions" (whatever that is), and the teachers would have more time for each student.

Anyway, if I started talking about what happened that day, I knew I'd cry. It was such a lousy day. I don't know how long I had been sulking, but suddenly we were pulling into the driveway. As we walked into the house, Mom asked me one more question: "Who wished you a happy birthday today?"

2

That was it. I had forgotten until then. It was my fifteenth birthday, and no one had remembered. I slammed the door, threw my book bag down, and ran straight up the stairs, tears streaming down my face. When I got to my room, I buried my face in my pillow. Mom tried to come up and talk to me, but all I could say was "Go away." I just wanted the day to end.

I must have fallen asleep because I woke up to Sticky licking my face and Mom calling me for supper.

"Come on, Sticky, let's go! It's suppertime," I said.

Gleefully, Sticky jumped off the bed and raced down the stairs.

"I made your favorite tonight, birthday girl!" Mom called from the kitchen.

Yes! I thought. *Chicken parmesan and salad. Yum!*

Suppertime used to be fun. My parents, Dakota, and I would sit around the table and share our day. Dakota always had something interesting and exciting to share, like the time her teacher brought the class to the beach to explore sea life firsthand, and she almost fell face-first into the tide pool trying to catch starfish. She did manage to get an awesome picture of about a dozen starfish clinging to the rocks, even if she did almost drown. Nothing cool like that ever happened to me.

Now, since Dakota had left for college, there were no more fun stories. It was just the three of us at the table, and all eyes were on me. I missed Dakota so much! Why did she have to leave anyway? Why couldn't she stay and attend the community college down the street?

Suddenly, I heard my dad saying rather gruffly "Lacy, answer your mother. She asked you a question."

"Huh? Sorry. I guess I'm not awake yet," I said.

"Lacy, how was your day?" asked Mom, smiling at me.

"Okay," I replied.

"How many kids are in your class? Is there anybody new this year?" she continued.

"No, Mom. All the same kids are there except Marie and Jade."

"Oh." She put her head down.

I thought that was it, that I could go back to eating my chicken, when Dad asked, "How are your classes? Did you find out if you have any special projects to do this year?"

My throat closed, and my stomach did a flip. I couldn't answer, so I looked down at my plate, intent on cutting my chicken into the tiniest pieces possible.

Dad asked me again, "Lacy, how are your classes?"

"Fine," I answered, still concentrating on my plate.

"What classes do you have?" Mom asked, trying to get the conversation going.

"Oh… math, English, history, same as always," I mumbled.

"Lacy, could you speak up? And please don't talk with food in your mouth," my mother chided.

"I said that I have all the same classes as usual," I snapped back.

My parents exchanged an aggravated look.

Then Dad said, "Lacy, that tone is disrespectful. Please remember that we are your parents."

"Sorry," I murmured.

Nobody said anything for a few minutes. The only sounds were those of forks and knives scraping against the dishes. I wanted to eat faster, to run away from the awkward silence.

"I was talking with Rachel's mom this afternoon. She mentioned that your grade has to do a science fair project this year. That sounds like fun, doesn't it?" Mom offered, breaking the silence.

Fun! Is she crazy? I was not looking forward to anything involving 1) writing a paper, 2) doing an experiment, and, worst of all, 3) presenting my project in front of everyone. What was fun about any of that?

"I suggested to Stephanie that maybe you and Rachel could be partners for the project," continued Mom.

What! I thought, horrified. *Me partner with Rachel?*

Suddenly, I couldn't eat any more. I put my fork down and started to get up from the table.

"Lacy, honey, you didn't finish your chicken. You love chicken parmesan. What's wrong?" asked Mom concerned.

"Wrong?" I cried. "You have to ask what's wrong? I have no friends! All of my friends left! Even Dakota ditched me!" I said, my throat burning as tears started to brim over my eyelids.

"It's my birthday, and no one even said, 'Happy birthday.'"

I sniffled as I fled the room. I ran back upstairs to the sanctuary of my room, with Sticky right behind me. She came over and started licking my face as I lay on my bed crying.

"I know, I know," I said through sobs. "I know you that you love me, Sticky."

A few minutes later, Mom knocked on my door.

"Lacy? Lacy, honey, can I come in?"

I didn't answer her. I just wanted to be left alone.

Mom poked her head through the doorway.

"Why don't you call Jade?" she asked.

Call Jade! How in the world could I do that? I'd been crying so hard I could barely breathe, never mind speak. Besides, she wouldn't want to talk to me anyway.

Mom tried again. "Lacy, it was Jade's first day today too. I bet she'd be happy if you called. She probably wants to tell you about her new school."

I was just about to scream, "No! She doesn't like me. She left me there all by myself with them!" when the phone started to ring.

Mom went to go answer it.

"Lacy, guess what? It's Jade! Come to the phone."

I jumped up and hurried to the phone. Maybe Jade still did want to be friends after all.

"Hi!" I said.

"Hi!" Jade answered. "I'm just dying to tell you about my day. I wanted to call you right when I got home, but we had to go shopping for school supplies."

"Oh," I said, trying to sound nonchalant, like I didn't care.

"Yeah, Lacy, you're not gonna believe it! There are so many kids in my class compared to our old class!"

"Really? How many?" I asked.

"Twenty-seven!"

"Twenty-seven! How many boys are there? Are they cute?" I asked, curious.

"Let me count … There's Doug, Josh, Chris, Jake, Zach, Michael, Luke, Matthew, and Jon. How many is that?"

"Nine boys."

"Those are the ones that I can remember their name. I think there's maybe three or four more."

Wow! I was so jealous. Twenty-seven kids in the class, and at least ten of them were boys.

"You said Jake and Michael …"

"No, they're not that Jake and Michael."

"How did you know I was thinking that?" I asked.

"Because I wondered the same thing when I saw their names on the desk."

"Hey, you didn't say if any of them are cute!"

"Lacy, it was only the first day! Okay, so Zach is kind of cute, and Chris likes to draw. He draws manga characters, just like Marie."

"That's cool."

"Yeah, I know. I'm going to have to tell Marie."

"What about the girls? Are they nice?"

"So far. Grace is new, like me. I sat with her and Serena at lunch today."

Jade and I talked and talked until Mom came to tell me that I needed to get ready for bed. I was so relieved that Jade had called. I had been worried that she would make new friends and forget me. I told her about the projects we had to do at our old school and the science fair. She said that she had to do a science fair project too. I told her about having to pick a partner for history and maybe also for the science project. She said she knew how I felt because there was an uneven number of kids in her class, and she didn't have a partner for the English assignment they were doing. Anyway, it wasn't just me who didn't have a partner! I loved talking with Jade. She always listened to what I had to say, and she didn't make me feel like a loser. Oh how I wished we still went to the same school!

Bam! Bam! Bam! I hated that stupid alarm clock! Whose idea was it to start school so early in the morning anyway? I hit the snooze button and put the pillow over my head.

"Five more minutes. All I need is just five more minutes."

Suddenly, everything was shaking. The pictures on my wall were trembling, my bed was rocking back and forth, and Sticky was howling!

Someone was yelling, and there were frantic footsteps. *An earthquake … It must be an earthquake.* Scared, I sat straight up to see Mom shaking my bed and yelling at me to get up. What? I looked over at the clock: 7:00 a.m.! No way! I had just hit the snooze button, hadn't I? But no. I had turned the alarm completely off. Seven o'clock! I would really have to hurry.

Seeing that I was finally awake, Mom went downstairs to fix my lunch, and I dashed into the shower. No time to daydream or sing. I couldn't be late on the second day. I quickly washed and rinsed my hair and jumped into my clothes. By 7:20, I was downstairs stuffing a bagel and cream cheese into my mouth.

Dad came into the kitchen.

"Wow! We're going to have to start calling you Flash!" he said.

"Huh?" I asked, bewildered.

"Well, you were in and out of the shower in a flash," he said, laughing.

"Ha-ha. Well, I have to get going," I said as I gulped a glass of milk. "Mom is already in the car."

I grabbed my backpack and my lunch and went out to the car.

"Oh good, you're ready," said Mom. "I thought I was going to have to honk the horn."

We pulled up to school at 7:55. Amazingly, I had a minute or two to arrange things in my locker. I was trying to be more organized since I had my own locker now. Last year, I shared a locker with Jade. I loved Jade. I mean she was my bestie, but sharing a locker was *not easy*. She would just throw her books in there any old way. Then she would tear apart the whole locker trying to find things.

I remember one day when she couldn't find her English paper. Everything lay strewn on the floor of the hallway—her books, my books, both our backpacks, papers everywhere, a couple of apples, a half-eaten pear, three bags of chips, her jacket, and my diary. Yes, my diary was lying there wide open for the whole world to read! In fact, that's what happened. Before I could get there, Rachel picked it up and started reading it *out loud*!

"Hey, everybody! Look what I found! It's Lacy's diary!"

So everybody had gathered around to listen while I tried desperately to grab it back from her. I must have looked so stupid, especially when she held it over her head so I had to jump for it! I was so upset I wanted to run away, but I needed to get that diary back before she got to the part about my crush.

I can still hear her now: "Ooh! Lacy likes somebody!"

Just as Rachel was about to reveal my secret crush, Kyle walked behind her, reached out his hand, and took the diary. Then, without saying a word or looking in it, he handed it back to me. As he walked away, I heard him tell his friend that that was why lockers had locks. Kyle, what a sweetie! He had saved me from total and utter embarrassment.

And Jade. What had Jade done? She threw everything back into the locker, of course. Then she went to find a teacher to help because, of course, there wasn't one around when you needed one.

Anyway, this year, nothing like that would happen. I was going to be totally organized. I had all of my books covered. I had a notebook and a binder for each subject, and they were all color coordinated. My science book was covered in green, so my notebook and binder for science were green too. Easy, right? I hoped so.

Now, I just had to figure out how to work the lock. This year, we all had combination locks. Last year, it was easy because I brought in a key lock from home. All I had to do was wear the key around my neck, and I didn't lose it. This year, I had to learn the combination. Mrs. Hart gave us the combination and lock the day before. Which way did it go again? Right, left, right or left, right, left? Argh! It was so frustrating. I really was bad at it. It took me so long to get it just right. I was always one or two places off, or I went past the number and had to start all over again.

Mrs. Hart smiled as we all went into the room for English. "Good morning, girls. Today we will start reading the American novel *To Kill a Mockingbird* by Harper Lee. Here is a list of vocabulary words from the first chapter that you will need to know."

Amanda rolled her eyes as she passed the papers back to Rachel, who did her best to look totally bored.

Mrs. Hart continued, "I'm sure that you all will find the story interesting. It is about the adventures of a boy and his younger sister, Scout, growing up in the South in the 1930s."

We took turns reading, and before I knew it, class was almost over.

"Your homework is to write three questions about what we've read so far. We'll discuss them together tomorrow," said Mrs. Hart.

Three questions? No problem, I thought.

Then, as I was walking to my locker to get my books for the next class, I heard it: "Is she kidding? She wants us to come up with three questions about that boring book. She must be crazy!" complained Amanda. "I don't have time for that. Volleyball practice is this afternoon."

Rachel and Laura nodded their heads in agreement, and then Kate chimed in, "The other teachers better not give us homework. They all know that we have volleyball today."

The day sped by, and before I knew it, it was lunchtime. I hated lunchtime. I knew that it would be the same as the day before. I would be sitting by myself with no friends to talk to. Maybe, if I took my time getting there, it wouldn't seem so long, and maybe no one would notice that I was all by myself. Good idea! I would just go to the restroom before lunch.

Unfortunately, I forgot that that's where the gang liked to hang out before lunch. Kate, Alyssa, Laura, and Aimee were already in there, brushing their hair and giggling.

Hoping that they would leave soon, I slipped into one of the stalls without them noticing.

They were talking about someone and laughing. I couldn't really hear what they were saying though because the faucet was on.

"Did you see?" Laura asked mockingly.

"See what?" responded Aimee.

"Hee-hee-hee! Her face! She looked like a clown!"

"Oh yeah!" Rachel said as she came out of another stall. "That was hilarious! She had cream cheese all over her face!"

"Are you sure it was cream cheese and not just pimples?" said Alyssa.

Then they were all laughing really hard.

"Seriously, I bet she never even washes her face!" added Laura.

That's when I reached up and felt the hard bits of cream cheese that had crusted all around my mouth. Oh no! I had eaten breakfast so fast that morning that I had literally shoved it into my face! Why hadn't Mom told me that I had cream cheese all over me?

"Rachel, can we turn the water off now?" asked Aimee.

"Sure, unless you're going to go pee. I hate the sound of peeing," Rachel answered.

Then they all laughed again and left for the lunchroom.

Finally, I was alone. I was so embarrassed. Everyone had seen me with cream cheese all over my face. *Oh, why am I such an idiot?* I ran to look in the mirror. There it was. Just like they had said. I even had some on my nose—and was that a piece of crusty cheese in my hair? I hoped Kyle hadn't seen me like that. What would he think?

I washed my hands and wiped the white crusty bits off of my face. I searched my bag for a brush with no luck. I ran my fingers through my hair, trying to fix the mess, but nothing worked. I would just have to walk around the rest of the day looking like I had stuck my finger in an electrical outlet.

Just a few minutes of lunch were left. I had to get moving if I was going to eat anything.

I hurriedly pushed the door open, and to my surprise, I almost slammed straight into Kyle. He was coming out of the boys' room at the same time. He smiled and headed for the lunchroom humming one of my favorite hymns, "Come Thou Fount of Every Blessing." The congregation had sung it in church on Sunday, and I had been singing it ever since. I guess I had been singing it subconsciously at school too. Yup! That must have been why Rachel told me to shut up when I was at my locker earlier.

Wow! Kyle must like that song too!

Note to Jade #2

Hi Jade!

I hope that you're having fun at school. What's it like having so many kids in class?

I'm so tired of the same old people in class. All they do is gossip and complain. Remember how they would make fun of Mrs. Strickland? Funny how she never noticed. She thought they really liked her, but they were always laughing at her. The girls at your new school don't do that, do they?

Of course, I looked like an idiot today. I went half the day with cream cheese all over my face! It was so embarrassing. I hope Kyle didn't notice. Hey, you know what my new favorite song is, right? Kyle was humming it today when I nearly ran into him again!

We have a lot of homework. Mr. Grimes said we have a lot to catch up on. We're learning how to multiply and add exponents again! Fortunately, if we get the problems right, we only have to do the odd numbers in the workbook. Alyssa and Kate are having to do the whole page though! Serves them right for not paying attention. I wonder if they'll get all the homework done since there is a volleyball practice today. Do they have volleyball at your new school?

Your bestie,
Lacy

Letter to Lacy

Hi Lacy,

So you know how I love mornings, right? Well, I was running late as usual and just threw on my clothes. When I got to school, I took off my jacket, and Serena looked at me funny. She just gave me a strange look and said, "Put your jacket back on—quick! Come to the restroom with me." I had no idea what she was talking about, but I followed her anyway. You know what? She told me when we got there that I had my shirt on inside out! Can you believe it? I would have been so embarrassed to walk around like that. I'm so glad she told me before anyone else noticed it.

I started drawing cartoon characters. Grace saw it and said it was good and showed it to Chris. He was so surprised that a girl likes manga. I wonder why. Have you been drawing anything lately? We are studying insects in science now, so I have to try to draw them. Blech! I hate bugs!

So, who do you eat lunch with now? Do ninth, tenth, and eleventh grades all have lunch together, same as last year? That is how it is here too. I sat with Jordan, Sarah, and Liz today. The boys sit at a different table, but Chris kept looking over at us. Sarah says that he has a crush on Liz.

Well, gotta go. Study hall is over.

Later,
Jade

The intercom crackled as Pastor Dave gave the daily announcements. "Good morning, students and staff. Thank you to all the students who tried out for our sports teams. Team lists are posted in the main hallway."

Laura and Alyssa were pretending to bump a ball as they made their way through the hall.

Rachel and Aimee were talking about the fun road trips the volleyball team always made. I could feel the scowl on my face, thinking I would be left out again.

Then I heard Tim laughing as he and Kyle weaved their way through the crowd, kicking a rolled-up ball of paper like a soccer ball. Just seeing Kyle smiling brightened my day, and I found myself smiling too. Kyle had such a great smile! No matter how sad I was feeling, his smile was like a gigantic rainbow that brightened the sky. I wondered if he knew.

Smiling to myself, I walked into art class with the image of Kyle's smiling face burned onto my retinas.

Buzz-buzz. Buzz-buzz. It was my cell phone vibrating. I had gotten a text. Well, class was about to begin, so it would have to wait. I didn't want my phone to be taken away.

Mrs. Peters was explaining the assignment. "Your mission today is to communicate the love you have for your favorite hobby through pictures and drawings only. You may not use any words. Express how you feel through the shapes you draw and the colors you choose."

Everyone looked at one another blankly. Their faces seemed to say, "Huh? What does she mean? A hobby?"

Thankfully, Mrs. Peters went on. "It can be anything that you like to do: sports, music, singing, reading, playing with your dog. Just make it interesting and try not to use conventional colors."

Then she showed us an example. She had drawn a picture of herself painting. She was outside under a tree with a paintbrush and easel; only the tree wasn't brown and green. It had yellow leaves and a red trunk. The sky in her picture wasn't blue but a deep purple. It looked gorgeous! I looked again and noticed that the painter in the picture was not only painting the canvas. She had two or three more arms and was painting the grass, the trees, and the sky! Wow! It was super cool! *It's too bad that Marie isn't here. She would love this project!* Art was her thing.

Usually I didn't like art class. I couldn't draw to save myself, but that seemed like a really neat project. I could do anything I wanted, and no one could tell me it was wrong! Now to decide on a hobby to show in the picture. I really still liked playing with my dolls even though everyone else in the class thought it was babyish. I loved styling their hair, dressing them in cute outfits, and creating short stories about them. The best was when I had them "act out" skits that I made up. It was fun to video those with my camera. Mom thought I was going to be a movie producer someday.

So, how am I going to show all this on a flat piece of paper? I wondered.

I looked around the room to see what everyone else was doing.

Laura was drawing what looked like clothes. That made sense since she was into fashion.

Amanda was making a bunch of different colored swirls on her paper. It looked pretty, but I had no idea what it was supposed to be.

Kate was concentrating on a detailed drawing of a ballerina. Wow! I wished I could draw like she could! Kate had always been incredible at drawing, and she'd been dancing for years, so her drawing a ballerina made perfect sense.

Rachel and Alyssa were hunched over their desks, working intently and whispering. Every once in a while, one of them would look up as if to make sure no one was watching them. I couldn't help but wonder what they were doing.

Hey! Were they working together? Mrs. Peters hadn't said anything about having a partner. It was supposed to be an individual assignment, wasn't it? I looked around again. No one else had a partner. I guessed I was safe. It was just Rachel and Alyssa being Rachel and Alyssa, doing what they wanted—again.

I decided to draw a picture of me as a hairdresser, styling my doll's hair. Doing their hair was always fun. I started drawing my favorite doll, Felicity, with her long copper-colored hair. She was standing next to her friend Elizabeth while I brushed her hair. Since the picture wasn't supposed to be exactly realistic, I made Elizabeth's hair a super bright neon yellow, glowing like the sun. Felicity's hair was so long that the luscious waves wrapped around her and fell gently to her feet. With my drawing skills, there was no way I could draw them in their outfits from the 1700s. It was a good thing I didn't have to. A simple skirt and blouse would work. I would decide on the colors later. In the upper left-hand corner of the paper, I drew a video camera. Well, I hoped Mrs. Peters would be able to tell that it was a video camera. To me, it looked more like a box with a circle stuck onto the right-hand side of it. The background would be purple like my room. I glanced up at the clock. Dang! There were only a few minutes left.

I raised my hand. "Mrs. Peters, do we have to finish the picture before the end of class? Mine isn't done yet."

She looked up from the desk. "No, Lacy. But please, everyone, turn in what you've done, and I'll pass them back for you to finish next class," she said.

I put my name on the back and got up to pass mine in. There was a rustle of papers and books and chairs scraping as everyone else got up too.

Aimee saw my picture and started to giggle. Amanda looked over then, too, and began to snicker.

I quickly put my picture face-down on the desk so that no one else would see.

Laura got to the desk next and, being the neatnik that she was, had to organize the small pile of papers, fixing them into a neat stack so that they were all going the same way. Unfortunately, she placed the pictures face-up—with guess whose picture on top!

As the bell rang, Alyssa and Rachel hurried to the desk to drop off their work. Of course, they saw my picture sitting there and cracked up laughing.

"Ha-ha-ha! I didn't know her hobby was wrestling!" said Alyssa.

"Yeah, I know!" Rachel laughed. "I don't know though. Maybe they're not wrestlers. Maybe it's supposed to be Amazon warriors. I mean, I think that one is a girl. Look at that hair. No—wait! It's Medusa!"

I picked up my books as fast as I could and headed to my locker. Why did they have to be so mean? So what if I couldn't draw perfectly like Kate! I was sure their drawings weren't much better than mine. I started to sulk. Who was I kidding? Everyone in the class was better at art than me. It was true. Every time I tried to draw a person, it either looked like a zombie or a deformed munchkin. I should have just stuck to making stick figures. Too bad Marie wasn't there. She would have helped me. She was a fantastic sketch artist. The year before, she won first place in the art fair for her comic strip.

My phone was buzzing again. I decided to check it before I got to class. It was a message from Marie, "Flying pancakes." That was all it said: "Flying pancakes." Then the second text was a smiley face. I could feel the smile creeping up on my face as my lips turned right side up. Marie had turned my frown upside down. What in the world did she mean, "Flying pancakes"? It didn't matter; it was Marie being Marie, being funny. I quickly texted her back, "?". Buzz-buzz. "I'm so-o-o bored! I just wanted to see what you'd say if I texted you something utterly ridiculous." Yup, that was Marie. I had learned to expect the unexpected.

Next, we had English. We were still reading *To Kill a Mockingbird*. It was pretty interesting. We found out that Jem and Scout had a neighbor, "Boo" Radley, that no one ever saw. Even though no one had seen him for years, they knew that he was still there because they saw that the shade in the window jerked when they walked by his house, and sometimes things in the yard had been moved around. Also, small presents, a whistle one day, a top the next, started appearing in the hollow tree next to Jem and Scout's house, which was next door to Boo Radley's. The children tried to imagine what Boo must look like—maybe a wolf or a vampire, since he never went out in the daylight.

I found myself wondering about Boo too. *Why doesn't he go outside? Why doesn't he talk to anyone? Is he lonely? Doesn't he have a job?* The biggest question though was, *What kind of a name is Boo? Why in the world is he called Boo?*

"Okay, ladies," instructed Mrs. Hart. "Work with your partner to answer the questions you each wrote for homework last night."

Partner work. I loathed working with a partner now that all of my friends had left. At least I didn't have to die of embarrassment this time because of not having a partner. Mrs. Hart started assigning us a weeklong partner because she wanted us all to work with everyone and not keep picking the same partner. That week, I was partners with Amanda. She was okay. Even though she hung out with Rachel and Alyssa, she usually wasn't mean to me like they were. She didn't really talk to me unless she had to though.

I moved over to the empty desk next to hers and got my homework out. I sat there for a couple of minutes waiting for her to get hers out.

Finally, I asked her if she had her questions. I hoped we could just exchange papers and answer the questions on our own, instead of having to actually talk to each other.

Amanda started ruffling papers, searching through her backpack.

I decided to get up and sharpen my pencil instead of sitting there like an idiot waiting for her.

As I turned to go back to my seat, I saw Rachel smirking as she dropped a folded piece of paper on my desk. I didn't dare look at it. I just shoved it in my bag.

Amanda couldn't find her homework that she swore she had done, so she quickly wrote out some questions. Let me tell you, her questions were not at all like mine. I wondered if she had been reading the book at all. I thought the questions were supposed to challenge us to think about what the story was about, what the author might be trying to tell the reader. That's what Mrs. Hart had said anyway. Amanda's questions were so basic: 1) What is the title of the book? 2) Who are the main characters? 3) Who is Boo Radley? I quickly answered Amanda's questions but then had to help her with my questions: 1) Why is the setting of the story important? 2) What do they find in the hollow of the tree? 3) Why is the title of the book important? What does it mean?

I wondered what that paper Rachel put on my desk said. Part of me wanted to know. Another part of me didn't because I suspected that whatever that paper had to say wouldn't be good. What I did know was that I wasn't going to look at it in class in front of them.

They had passed a note to Marie last year, except it wasn't a note; it was more like a threat. Marie was seriously upset. We all told her that she should show her mom or the teacher, but she wouldn't do it. Her mom was way too busy with her baby brother and working two jobs. There was no way Marie wanted to worry her mom. Instead, she would always tell me and Jade how mean the other girls were to her. Poor Marie! Poor us! I got so tired of hearing her complain.

Mrs. Hart was saying something. "You have all come up with some very good questions. Let's discuss this one: 'Why is the title of the book important? What does it mean?' Does anyone remember any mention of a mockingbird in the story?"

There was total silence as all the girls stared blankly back at Mrs. Hart. I looked up at the clock. Hooray. There were only a few minutes left. Mrs. Hart must have noticed the time, too, because she quickly said that our homework was to find the passage on page 103 that talked about the mockingbird and to tell how it was a metaphor for the story.

Then the bell rang. Phew! Normally, I liked English, but I was glad it was over for the day!

We had gym next. Everybody else hurried to their lockers, grabbed their gym bags, and headed for the locker room. Not me. Gym was the worst. Whoever decided that there should be a class to show everybody just how ugly, awkward, and uncoordinated you are was really incredibly mean. I would have skipped gym if I could have, but it was a requirement. If I didn't participate, I wouldn't graduate. I slowly got my gym bag and went to the girls' locker room. Everybody else was already changed and on their way into the gym.

I got my uniform out and was about to change when I remembered the note Rachel left on my desk. Since no one else was there, I decided to look at it. It was a sketch of me with food and zits all over my face. I was drawn to look very small, with large eyes and tears streaming down my face as I clutched a rag doll and ran screaming from a volleyball that was humongous. I mean it was three times bigger than I was drawn in the picture. I sat there in disbelief. I wish I could say that I was shocked, but I wasn't. I knew that they didn't like me. I could feel a lump growing in my throat, and my eyes started to swell with tears. *They're right! I'm just a big baby!* There was no way I could go to gym class. I sat there, hurt and alone, sniffling and wiping my eyes. I was a loser. I had no friends because I was lame. It wasn't fair. Why, oh, why did all my friends have to leave?

As I sat there on the hard wooden bench crying to myself, I remembered again the drawing that Rachel had given Marie last year. Then I remembered other things too. I thought about how Marie had always complained to us about how the other girls picked on her. This must have been how she had felt, but Marie wasn't a loser! Marie was really cool and fun to be around. She was always joking and laughing about something.

Oh, no! I guessed I had been mean too. When she needed me to listen and help her out, I just got aggravated and ignored her. Then, even worse, when Mrs. Strickland had asked me once if Rachel was bullying her that day at lunch, I had said no. Sure I hadn't seen Rachel making fun of her then, but she sure did whenever she could! Why hadn't I said something? Why didn't I tell her about the knife picture?

I began to cry harder. The tears were streaming down my face, dripping on the horrible picture of me. I crumpled it up and shoved it in my bag before I ran to the toilet to throw up. I was a loser! I was such a coward! I should have told Mrs. Strickland the truth. Now, because I was scared or didn't care enough, now I had no friends.

Just then, the girls came back into the locker room.

Mrs. Jones was with them.

"Oh there you are, Lacy. Are you all right?" she asked.

I told her that I had an upset stomach and that I had just vomited, so she had me go the office and call my mom to go home. Thank goodness! Thank God I was going home.

As soon as I was by myself again, I texted Jade.

"Jade, you won't believe what Rachel and Alyssa did to me! They drew this horrible picture of me with zits all over my face being crushed by a volleyball. Of course they had to make fun of me still playing with dolls too. They are so-o-o-o mean!"

A few minutes later, I heard my phone buzz. It was Jade, texting back: "You're right. They are really mean! Remember how they drew that knife picture and gave it to Marie?"

"Yeah, I know. She was really upset. She should have told someone about it," I replied.

"I know," Jade went on. "I kept encouraging her to tell her mom. She did finally tell Mrs. Strickland that Rachel was bullying her though."

My eyes got big when I read that last text. Marie had told Mrs. Strickland! I didn't know that.

"She did? When did she do that?" I asked.

"In December, before Christmas break," she explained. "Mom had come to pick me up. We had decided to wait with her until her mom got there. Suddenly she jumped up and ran back inside for homework she had forgotten in her locker. When she came out of the building, she was so happy! She burst through the doors calling, 'I did it! I did it! I told Mrs. Strickland how Rachel has been bullying me!' I think she was relieved that she had finally told."

"I didn't know that."

"Yup. Then a couple of days before Christmas, you remember when the gang was picking on Marie again? I told my mom, and she asked me what I was going to do about it. She emailed Mrs. Strickland, and then we both went in to talk with her and the other teachers about it."

Wow! They had actually told. Marie and Jade had actually told what was happening. I didn't know what to think. I didn't know how to feel. My mom always told me to stay out of things that didn't concern me. "Did it happen to you? It's none of your business then. Stay out of it! Don't get caught in the middle," is what she always said.

The phone buzzed again. It was still Jade.

"And do you know what? When we were talking with the teachers, Mrs. Strickland called me a liar! She said what I was saying didn't happen because she had already asked you, and you said nothing was going on! Thanks a lot, Lacy, for backing me up!"

My heart fell into the pit of my stomach. A liar? I couldn't believe it! Jade, a liar? There was no way. That was so wrong, and it was all my fault that they thought that Jade was lying. I started to cry again, thinking how my cowardice had hurt Marie and Jade. Jade was my best friend! How could I have hurt my best friend!?

Buzz. Buzz. The phone was going off again.

"Are you still there?"

"Uh huh. I'm sorry. I didn't know that I got you in trouble," I typed between sobs.

"Oh, no problem. My mom pointed out to the teachers that Mrs. Strickland already did know that Marie was being bullied. She remembered how Marie had been so proud of herself and relieved to have told Mrs. Strickland about what was going on. My mom was a witness."

"Are you mad at me?"

"I was really mad at Mrs. Strickland for calling me a liar! Why would I lie? Why would anyone make that up? Besides, isn't lying against the Ten Commandments?"

"How did you have the courage to tell?"

"I decided that I had to tell. Remember the year before when Marie-Beth came to the school? Do you remember how the gang treated her? She was so upset that she quit eating!"

"Yeah, I remember. I felt bad for her."

"Do you remember what Mrs. Strickland said then? Even if we hadn't bullied her, we were just as responsible, just as guilty because we hadn't said anything. We didn't do anything to defend her. So I knew that I had to say something when it happened to Marie."

My stomach was all in knots. I did remember that. What a coward I was! I had failed all of my friends when they needed me most. I cried most of the afternoon. No wonder all my friends had left me! I didn't deserve to have any friends.

No matter that I felt like my world was ending, the sun set and rose again the next day. The promise of a new day, a chance to change things, put them right. That's what Grandma had always said. She was always so bubbly and happy. I wished that I could be more like her right then. All I could do was think about how miserable I was. I would have to go back to school and be with them. They were all so obnoxious and self-absorbed. I knew that no one even cared that I was sick the day before. *Can I really make it through the whole school year?* I wondered.

I managed to drag myself out of bed and into the shower. I loved showers. The feel and sound of the warm water rushing over me cleansed me; yes, somehow it cleared my head and opened my heart. I did my best thinking and singing in the shower. I would stay in there all day if I didn't run out of hot water. I sang about life, love, lost love, God, and my dreams. All of my innermost thoughts and feelings came pouring out of me like a glorious waterfall.

> The sun comes up
> It's a new day dawning
> It's time to sing Your song again
> Whatever may pass
> And whatever lies before me
> Let me be singing
> When the evening comes

Yup, "Ten Thousand Reasons." It was one of my favorites. Sometimes I even wrote my own songs. Maybe one would be a hit one day. Who knew?

I barely managed to make it to school on time.

As I was hurrying through the door, Kyle brushed past me on his way to homeroom.

"Oh!" I squeaked.

"Hey! Sorry!" he called as he quickly strode away.

Everyone seemed to be staring at me as I entered the building and made my way to my locker. Why were they all looking at me? I opened my locker and instantaneously saw why. Not only was my hair still wet from my ultra-long, hot shower, my face was bright red and pink like a splotchy tomato from the steam. I looked again. Oh no! My eyes were still puffy from all the crying I had done the day before. I looked horrendous! What was I going to do? I really wanted to run away so no one could see me. Maybe I could just put my bag over my head? Doh! Then I would look like a complete idiot.

Brrrng! That was the warning bell. Maybe if I just wrapped my scarf up around my neck more, no one would notice. I grabbed my books and ran to homeroom just as the door was closing.

Pastor Dave was on the intercom reading the verse of the day. He was reciting Jesus's words from Matthew 25:45, "Then shall he answer them, saying, Verily I say unto you, Inasmuch as ye did it not to one of the least of these, ye did it not to me."

I was listening, trying to decide if this was any different from the verse in Luke 6:31, "Do unto others as you would have them do unto you." Then I was distracted by the chatter in the room.

"Oh, yeah! Spirit week!" Rachel sang out. "Hey, Alyssa, what are we going to do for twin day?"

All the girls were chattering excitedly, making plans with each other for twin day, sports day, Bible-character day, and fake-an-injury day. I sat quietly by myself. No one wanted to plan anything with me.

The bell rang. Homeroom was over, and it was time to go to chapel. We were having a special chapel today. A speaker from Pensacola College, Mr. Jacobs, had come to speak to us.

We filed into the sanctuary and sat with our class. As we got settled in our seats, I happened to notice Kyle looking over. Tim motioned for Kyle to come sit next to him, in the pew right in front of me! I could feel myself start to smile, and my cheeks turned pink as Kyle made his way over. I had to look away before he saw.

Pastor Dave started with a prayer. Mr. Jacobs spoke about devoting your life to Christ and how choosing a college could fit into a Christ-centered life. Then he told us kind of a funny story about himself. He explained how, when he was in high school, he really liked a girl, Jayne, but was too shy to tell her. So he hung out with his friends, played sports, did his schoolwork, and life went on as he wistfully looked over at her and dreamt. Graduation day came, and everyone left for college, work, or the military. Mr. Jacobs went down to Pensacola Christian, and to his great joy, he found that Jayne had decided on the same school. He could still happily watch her from afar! Only he began to realize that not only was she more and more beautiful, but other guys were noticing her beauty too. Finally, he got up the courage to speak to her and ask her for a date. Now, they're happily married! His parting advice for the guys, "Don't wait years to tell the girl that you like her. It was truly a blessing that everything worked out for us, but think of all the time I wasted and the moments we could have shared. Don't let your fear overcome you. Be courageous!"

So many thoughts were swimming around in my head: Mr. Jacob's story, the words of Jesus, and those of Luke in the Bible. "Be courageous," and "Do unto others as you would have them do unto you." Those made sense to me. I needed to be more brave and do what I knew was right.

I should act toward others how I wanted to be treated, with caring and respect.

But what exactly did Jesus's words mean? "Verily I say unto you, Inasmuch as ye did it not to one of the least of these, ye did it not to me." It sounded backward to me. Why was the word *not* in there? The words seemed to be saying to do something and not to do something at the same time.

Just then, I realized that Pastor Dave was saying something. "The cooler weather will be approaching soon and will be here before we know it. All of us love winter, right? Who here does a winter sport like skiing or ice-skating?"

About twenty hands shot up in the air.

"Well, then," Pastor Dave continued, "you all know how important it is to dress warmly for these activities. This year, the school has been asked to help those who don't have the resources to buy winter clothes get ready for the cold. Shelters usually receive enough sweaters and jackets, but things like socks are forgotten. We are asking each of you to be a servant of the Lord by buying a small bag of socks to be donated to the homeless. Remember Jesus's words: 'Inasmuch as ye did it not to one of the least of these, ye did it not to me.' In other words, 'Whatever you failed to do for one of my brothers or sisters, no matter how unimportant they seemed, you failed to do for me.' We are to help others, including the least among us, as if that person was Jesus. For, by not helping, we are hurting, and we are hurting Jesus, who suffered and died because of our sin."

So, that's what it means then! I had been afraid that it somehow contradicted the other verse, but it didn't. They worked perfectly together! The words kept running through my mind the rest of the day: "Whatever you failed to do for one of my brothers or sisters, no matter how unimportant they seemed, you failed to do for me." *I failed! I did. I really did.* I had failed Marie. I had failed Jade. I had failed myself, and I had failed Jesus! I should have stood up and told the truth no matter how hard it seemed. Somehow it surely would have been easier than the way things had turned out.

Was there anything I could do now, or was it too late? Had I already lost my friends and my best friend? I was surprised that Jade even talked to me at all.

"Lacy, hurry up! You're going to be late!" called Mom from the bottom of the stairs.

I quickly threw my sweater on, slipped into my chinos, and headed down the stairs.

I grabbed my book bag and coat on the way out the door and plopped into the passenger seat.

"Here I am! Let's go!" I announced as I adjusted the seat belt.

I looked over at Mom to see why she hadn't started the car yet. She was sitting there staring at me with a stunned expression, not saying a word.

"Mom, let's go! You said yourself I'm going to be late!"

Then Mom burst out laughing uncontrollably.

"Why are you laughing?" I asked, fearing the worst.

"You … look … like … like … you're in a horror movie!" said Mom between fits of laughter. "The makeup … is just so … so … ha-ha-ha!" She couldn't control herself.

"Yes, Mom, it's spirit week. Don't you remember that today is fake-an-injury day?"

All she could do was nod up and down as she tried to stop laughing.

"Hey! I'm supposed to be hurt here! Why are you laughing at an injured person?" I joked.

I guess I had done a good job. I had decided to pretend that I had gotten electrocuted, so my hair was standing straight up, and I had put on brown and black charcoal-like makeup to look like I had gotten toasted. I had even taped a toaster to my sweater! I hoped I was the only one to think of that. Everyone else would have crutches or a broken arm. Not me! I was original.

Finally, Mom regained her composure, and we headed to school.

As we pulled into the parking lot, I saw that I was right. Pretty much everyone else had crutches, a sling, or maybe even fake blood, but nobody looked like me.

"Wow, Lacy! Looking good!" said Alyssa as I entered the building.

Rachel and Aimee nodded in agreement.

I didn't know what to say. I could never tell if they were being mean or not. Then I rounded the corner and saw it—the reminder about picture day. No way! It couldn't be, but it was! Today was picture day, and I looked like this! Now, everyone would remember me looking like some burnt-up weirdo with my hair sticking straight up.

I wanted to crawl into my locker and hide. Who in the world plans picture day and spirit week at the same time? Instead of trying to hide in my locker, I bolted for the door, hoping that Mom hadn't left yet, since she had been chatting with Mrs. Strickland. But, as if in slow motion, my hand opened the door just in time to see her pull away and turn the corner out of the schoolyard.

My brain screamed, "No! Come back!" as I stood there soundless and motionless.

I don't know how long I stood there, but suddenly Mr. Grimes was telling me that the warning bell had rung and I'd better hurry to class.

With my eyes stinging as they started to well up with tears, I moved on.

As I snatched my books out of my locker, I was sure I heard the other girls snickering.

"Oh, my! Lacy's finally wearing makeup!"

"Yeah, she looks stunning."

"She's so hot! Can't wait to see the pictures!"

Why can't they just shut up? I thought. I felt bad enough that I had forgotten and looked so stupid.

Then I felt someone tap me on the shoulder. I whipped around, ready to tell Rachel, or Alyssa, or whichever one of the girls exactly what I thought, but as I started to open my mouth, I realized that I could have been looking in a mirror. The person looking back at me had his hair sticking straight up with brown and black makeup all over his face and some fake blood too. Then, when he smiled with his bright blues eyes twinkling, I noticed that he had a tooth missing too. I smiled, then laughed, and so did he. The bell rang then, so I just waved shyly and glided, as if on a cloud, all the way to class.

My reverie was broken by Mrs. Hart telling us something. I decided that it must be important because the other girls stopped chatting to pay attention.

"Tomorrow, we will have a new student joining our class," she began.

I could see the looks of anticipation and hopefulness on everybody's face. I turned just in time to see Rachel mouth the words "A new boy?" to Alyssa, who gave her a thumbs-up.

I quickly prayed that it would be a new girl. Ever since I could remember, I always prayed for new girls to come to the school. How wonderful it would be to have a new best friend! Then I wouldn't have to eat lunch alone.

"Her name is Faith, and she just moved here from Georgia. Tomorrow will be her first day with us. I'm sure you will all give her a warm welcome," finished Mrs. Hart.

Yay! It is going to be a new girl! I could feel my lips turn up into a smile. As I scanned the room, though, I could tell that my classmates were not as enthused as I was to have another girl in class. Rachel and Alyssa looked disappointed, and the other girls didn't seem to care at all.

All evening, I wondered what the new girl would be like. What would she look like? Would she have blond hair, brown, straight hair, or wavy reddish-brown hair like mine? Would she be tall or short? I hoped that she liked to sing. It would have been great to have someone to sing with again. I really missed running out to recess and making up songs like Jade and I used to do. Hopefully she had a dog too, or at least liked dogs. It would be fun if she did. Then we could take Sticky for long walks and talk. As long as she didn't make fun of Sticky for being tiny. Sticky hated that. She almost bit a boy once for saying that she wasn't "a real dog." She wanted to show him that she was!

Even though I couldn't stop myself from wondering about Faith, I decided that I had to keep my ruminations to myself. If I mentioned it to Mom, she would ask me a million questions when I got home from school. I couldn't tell Jade because, well, *awkward*! She had already made a ton of new friends at her new school, and I was stuck eating lunch by myself. How could I tell her how excited I was for a new friend? I guess we were still friends, but I didn't want her to think I was a loser.

I wished Dakota was there. Dakota and I used to tell each other everything.

Morning finally arrived, and I hopped out of bed with a spring in my step, anticipating what the day would be like. Today was twin day, but I didn't have anyone to coordinate outfits with. Normally I would have been self-conscious about that, but that day I didn't care. I didn't have to worry about matching anyone or fitting in. I decided that I would make up for my horrific appearance yesterday by putting in some extra effort. Usually, I would ask my fashionista sister, Dakota, for advice. She would always laugh when I tried to put an outfit together, saying things like, "No, never put stripes and florals together," or "Why are you putting on your high-tops with that fancy dress? Yuck!"

She could always put together a killer outfit. She was one of those girls who not only knew the basics of creating an ensemble, she differentiated between subtle shades of color. I remembered when she went Goth. Her wardrobe had to be all black. Really black. Black-black. I didn't even know that there were different shades of black until she showed me. It just wouldn't do if her shirt was brown-black, her skirt was blue-black, and her sweater was green-black. They all at least had to be the same shade of black. Thank goodness she was only Goth for a week!

Oh well, maybe I had stored some of her style tips somewhere in my scattered brain.

Okay, I thought. *I'll just throw on a dress and some shoes, definitely not sneakers.*

I rifled through the clothes in my closet, looking for a dress.

"No, not the red one. That one makes my face look blotchy."

I kept looking.

"The light green one with the flowers on it? No, I look like I'm six years old in that one.

"How about this royal blue dress with the scoop neckline?"

I pulled it off of the hanger and tried it on for the first time since forever. It looked okay—not too long, not too short.

I walked over to the mirror.

Oh, no! I couldn't wear that! I had a minefield of zits on my chest. No wonder I never wore that one.

I threw the dress on my bed with the others I had rejected.

Then I heard Mom yelling up the stairs to me, "Lacy, are you ready? It's almost time to leave for school."

Oh no! I had lost track of the time, and I still wasn't dressed.

"No!" I yelled back. "Don't worry! I'll hurry!"

Quickly, I grabbed my favorite tie-dye skirt and white peasant top out of the closet. Dakota had given me the skirt for my birthday, and I loved it! It was purple, turquoise, and white.

As I passed the mirror on the way out of my room, I realized I hadn't even brushed my hair yet, but I could hear Mom honking the horn. I snatched my brush and some hair ties and rushed to the car.

Mom was about to scold me for running late when she looked over at me. Her face softened, and she said in a surprised tone, "My, don't you look nice today! Something special at school?"

"What? No," I answered as I pulled the brush through my tangles, trying not to wince.

"What do you think?" I asked as we left the driveway. "A French braid or a side braid?"

"A side braid is always pretty," Mom answered.

I was just putting the finishing touches on my hair when we pulled into the school parking lot.

Just as Mom pulled up to the door to drop me off, a light blue minivan pulled up behind us. A girl and a boy got out of the car slowly, as if unsure what to do next. Then I saw that the car had a Georgia license plate.

Of course! I realized. *This must be the new girl in my class, Faith, and the boy is probably her brother.*

"Hi!" I said with a big smile. "My name is Lacy."

The girl smiled back. "Hi!" she said. "My name is Faith, and this is my brother, Caleb. We're new here."

"I know," I said. "Our English teacher told us yesterday that you'd be here today."

Faith smiled even more, and we headed into the school together.

"You're in my class," I continued. "It's right over here."

Caleb waved bye and went down the hall to his class as we entered our homeroom.

"There's an empty desk next to mine," I said. "You can sit there."

"Thanks!" she answered.

"Brrr. Is it always this cold here?" Faith asked.

"Cold?" I repeated incredulously. It was only October, and there hadn't even been a frost yet.

"Yes. Aren't you cold?" she queried as she rubbed her hands together for warmth.

It was difficult for me to believe that anyone could be cold, especially this girl who looked so tan and healthy.

"No. Why should I be cold?" I asked, surprised.

"Oh! It's just that back home in Georgia, I mean, it's still seventy-five degrees," she explained.

"Really? Wow! That *is* warm! We're glad that it's almost fifty degrees here in the mornings. Don't worry though. It will probably make it up to seventy degrees by the afternoon since it is a sunny day."

Faith looked a little worried when I said that and murmured as the bell rang, "Oh! I'll have to get a sweater."

Mrs. Hart came into the room then and hurried over to welcome Faith. "Oh, there you are, dear! So glad to see you. Class, this is our new student that I was telling you about yesterday. Faith and her family just moved here from Georgia. I am sure that she will appreciate your help getting acquainted with the school."

All eyes turned to Faith as Mrs. Hart was speaking. Most of the girls were just being polite, but Rachel and Aimee were looking at her haughtily, with disdain in their eyes. They were looking at Faith, weren't they? Or maybe they were looking at me! I mean, they really hadn't even met Faith yet. How could they already not like her?

Before I knew it, homeroom was over, and the rest of the girls had flocked around Faith excitedly talking all at once. I knelt down to pick up my books, and in that instant, the crowd whisked her out of the room and away down the hall. Quietly, I went to the next class by myself.

I always liked having new girls in class. You know, so that there would be someone else to hang out with instead of just Jade and I. Also, it helped even things up so it wasn't the six of them versus the two of us! Only now Jade wasn't there. I felt like it was just me against the world. I had hoped that I could make friends with the new girl. Everything had just seemed to fall into place that morning. What had happened? Why didn't Faith wait to walk with me to the next class?

As I made my way to math, I thought about last year when Marie was new to the school. I thought she was cool, and I liked her, but Jade was, and would always be, my best friend. Jade and I were tight, and I was sure that nothing and no one could change that—until that one day at lunch. I had set my lunch bag down next to Jade's and went to the counter to buy some chips. When I came back, I saw that my bag had been moved and Marie was in my seat! She couldn't do that! Jade and I were besties. We always sat next to each other. She was my best friend. Marie would just have to find someone else. I told her that I was sitting there already and that she had to move. But she wouldn't! She defiantly sat there and told me, "No!" Then she tried to smooth it over by saying something about the three of us all being best friends, but I knew better.

Every year, a new girl would come to school and want to be best friends with Jade. I mean, I knew she was great—she was my best friend—but why her and not me? I could tell that they only tolerated me so that they could hang out with Jade. No, I wasn't going to let it happen. I wasn't going to share Jade only to lose her in the end. I needed her too much. It was then that I had decided that no one else could sit next to Jade, ever—not at lunch, not in chapel, not even when we went on field trips. Obviously, people didn't understand what *best friend* meant. When someone or something was the best, they were the top—the *one* and *only*, superior in a way. It was impossible to have *two* best friends. So, I made sure that Marie understood, saying, "No, you can't be my best friend because Jade is!"

Marie and Jade just stared and gave each other a funny look when I said that. Hurt and upset, I sat and ate lunch by myself that day. After that, I made sure I always sat next to Jade and went to school every day, even if I was sick. I was so worried that Jade would become best friends with Marie that I made sure never to be absent because I didn't want them to do anything without me! There was no way that I was going to let Marie take away my best friend.

I trudged into science class just as Mrs. Strickland was closing the door.

"Good morning, class!" she said cheerily. "Have you all decided on a science project?" she asked as she handed a piece of paper to each student.

Aimee raised her hand. "Mrs. Strickland, we didn't know that that was due today," she said resolutely.

All the other girls nodded in agreement.

"Oh, dear, it was on the packet that I passed out the first day of school."

Rachel raised her hand then and said sweetly, "But, Mrs. Strickland, we still don't know if we can have a science fair partner."

"Well, let me see …" Mrs. Strickland thought aloud. "There are only seven of you in the class, so …"

Alyssa's hand shot up, and she said, "Mrs. Strickland, there are eight of us now that Faith is here."

"Oh, that's true! Well, then, I'll give you some time now to choose a partner and discuss what you want to do for a project. Each group will have to list three possible science fair projects. This way, there won't be a problem if two groups pick the same topic. Someone will just have to choose one of their other options."

All the girls immediately paired up with their friends, leaving Faith and me sitting by ourselves on opposite ends of the room.

Mrs. Strickland walked over to Faith to give her the information packet.

I noticed that Faith looked a little scared, so I went over to sit with her.

"Hi!" I said.

"Hi!" she answered.

"I guess we're partners," I continued, trying to smile.

She looked at the thick packet, her eyes wide.

"Have you ever done this before?" she asked.

"Yeah, we had to do a project last year too, but I don't think it was as complicated. Don't worry. We can come up with something cool," I replied.

"I hope so," said Faith. "I'm not usually into science."

We talked about the things we liked and brainstormed for the rest of the hour. Of course, we thought of making a volcano erupt and making crystals, but everybody did those. We wanted to be original, or at least for the project to be interesting. The next idea we had was to see the best way to keep food fresher longer. It sounded doable but very boring. I suggested we try an experiment about dogs. We could use Sticky for the experiment. We thought about this a little while. Sticky already knew some tricks, so teaching her to do tricks wouldn't exactly work, would it? Would we need to try teaching other dogs the same tricks? What would be the control part of the experiment? Would other people, family members, inadvertently ruin the experiment by teaching the dog tricks or by giving it treats when they weren't supposed to? Nope, too many variables there. Then we thought of some sort of experiment involving plants. We could try growing flowers or tomatoes or something using different types of food or soil or water. We would have to be sure that there was only one variable though, or we wouldn't truly be able to measure what we were testing.

Just as we were discussing this, Mrs. Strickland walked by. "That's right!" she said. "Remember to be sure that the question you are asking can be answered and is quantifiable. In other words, be careful to have only one variable that is measurable."

Well, at least we were on the right track with understanding the scientific method. Now we just had to have a topic or maybe just a good question. *That's right!* The whole point of doing the experiment was to answer a question.

"Hey! Why don't we start by making a list of questions we have?" I asked. "You know, things we're interested in finding out."

Faith agreed.

Hopefully, we could turn at least one of the questions into a great project.

Scientific Questions

1. Why is the sky blue?
2. Why do dogs pant?
3. Does vinegar clean better than detergent?
4. What is more acidic, tomato sauce or lemon juice?
5. Which moisturizer works better? Why?
6. Which nail polish dries faster? Which nail polish lasts longer / doesn't chip? Why?
7. Who is stronger, boys or girls?
8. What grows better, organic plants or conventional plants?
9. Is being left-handed an advantage or a disadvantage? Does it matter? What about being ambidextrous?
10. Does the way you're dressed affect the way other people treat you?

We came up with ten questions. Now we had to narrow this list down to three possible science experiments. We had to have some idea of how to answer the question. The third question looked pretty easy. All we had to do was pick maybe three or four different detergents or dish liquids and compare how well they cleaned to vinegar. We wrote that one down on the short list to give to Mrs. Strickland.

Faith thought question number seven looked like fun. "Yeah, we could have everyone try to pick up my brother's weights." She chuckled.

"He thinks he's *so* strong, but I'm the one who had to carry the boxes of books upstairs," she added as she flexed her arm muscle.

I agreed that it would be fun to test everyone's strength. We wrote that one down too.

We had to choose one more to give to Mrs. Strickland.

"Are you left-handed?" Faith asked.

"No. Are you?"

"Actually, I'm not, but my brother and my parents are. Weird, huh?"

"Yeah, that is different," I answered. "I wonder why that is."

I had never thought about that before. Everybody in my family was a righty, except for Dakota. She was so lucky! She could write with both hands. I started to look around to see who was a righty or a lefty. Aimee and Rachel were both using their left hands. Laura was writing with her right hand. Suddenly, I wondered if Kyle was a righty or a lefty.

"Let's make that question our first choice," I suggested.

Instantly, a thousand questions popped into my head: What makes us become a righty versus being a lefty? Who is smarter, lefties or righties? Are more people left-handed or right-handed? Does being a lefty or a righty affect personality? If a person is left-handed, are they automatically ambidextrous?

Everybody turned in their choices to Mrs. Strickland as the bell rang.

"I will look these over and let you know what your project will be," she said as we gathered up our books to leave.

The day sped by, and soon it was time for lunch. I grabbed my sandwich out of my locker and moved toward the cafeteria. Hopefully, I could get Faith's attention and sit with her.

Just then, I saw the group of girls arriving from the bathroom. Kate, Aimee, Rachel, and Alyssa came in with Faith, laughing and giggling. Without noticing me, they plopped down at their usual table together, the conversation never slowing down. I could hear bits and pieces of what they were saying.

"Cool, you do ballet too. I love to dance."

"Is that your brother over there? Hey, he's cute!"

"Why did you move?"

"Too bad that you had to get stuck with Lacy for the science project. She's boring. Yeah, and she still plays with dolls."

Faith had been talking and answering their questions, but I noticed that she had a funny look on her face when they mentioned me. Then she looked around as if she was wondering where I was, like she just noticed that I wasn't there. I quickly shoved the rest of my food into my lunch bag and hurried to the restroom. I did not want her to see me sitting there by myself like a loser! Why were they all so mean anyway? It wasn't fair!

Buzz-buzz. Buzz-buzz. My phone was vibrating. Through blurry eyes, I fumbled for my phone. It was Jade! "Just got my science project. Cool topic. Call me."

I started to smile. *At least one person likes me*, I thought.

Mom picked me up right on time after school.

"Jump in. I have to go to the craft store," she said.

"Okay!" I said with a smile.

I loved going to the craft store. There was always interesting stuff there. When I was little, I used to love to get the teeny tiny teddy bears for twenty-five cents. Then I was into painting and doll clothes, and now I always went to the jewelry section. Jade's mom was into making custom jewelry. I helped sometimes when I went over to their house. It was so much fun picking out the beads and designing the jewelry! I wished my mom liked that sort of stuff, but she said that wearing a lot of jewelry was nonsense and made you look cheap. Mom was blessed with natural beauty though; she didn't need a lot of jewelry or makeup to look pretty. How I wished I was more like my mom with her perfect skin! But no, I had dad's skin, oily. Anyway, we were going to the craft store.

"Why are we going to the craft store?" I asked.

"We have to get supplies for making caramel apples," she said with a grin. "The fall festival is this Sunday, and I volunteered us to run the snack table."

I couldn't believe it. It was time for the fall festival already! I had been so busy that I'd hardly noticed the cool, crisp feel of the air and the leaves beginning to change from green to a glorious range of vibrant shades of red, burnt orange, and glowing gold. Fall was my favorite time of year. Besides the beauty of nature, it was sweater weather, not too hot and not too cold yet, just right for doing fun things outside like hay rides and apple picking.

Last weekend, Jade, Marie, and I went to a corn maze. It was a blast! Of course Mom had to come too, but we split up and lost her in the maze. We finished the maze three times before she even got to the end! She claimed that she was looking for us in the maze, but I thought that that was just an excuse.

"We're running the snack table!" I exclaimed happily. "Wow! This is gonna be fun! Can I ask Jade and Marie to help?"

"I don't see why not," Mom answered enthusiastically, "as long as you all are actually helping and not just fooling around. Isn't there a new girl in your class? You could invite her along too."

Mom looked at me when I didn't answer.

"What's the matter? Isn't she nice?"

"I guess," I mumbled.

"Why? Haven't you talked to her yet?" asked Mom.

"Of course I have!" I snapped back without thinking. "We're partners for the science fair."

Mom tried to stay upbeat even though I could tell that she hadn't liked my tone of voice. "Oh, good! Do you know what the project is yet?"

"Mrs. Strickland said that she will tell us after she looks over everybody's choices," I answered, trying not to think about what happened at lunch.

"Well, you should definitely invite the new girl to help this weekend. That way, you can get to know her better. What's her name?"

"Mom, just lay off, okay? I already have friends! They're named Jade and Marie!" I wanted to scream as the anger and humiliation grew inside of me. Why was my mom always telling me what to do? I could handle this myself. I was not in elementary school anymore!

We went to the craft store, but it wasn't as fun as usual. We didn't browse the scrapbooking section or even the aisle with doll accessories. Mom whisked us in and out, only buying what was absolutely necessary.

I called Jade and Marie as soon as we got home. I was so happy to talk to both of them. It was just like old times. I was laughing and giggling when Mom poked her head in the door.

"Who are you talking to?" she asked.

"Jade and Marie, of course!" I answered.

"At the same time?" Mom wondered out loud.

"Yup! Isn't technology great?" I answered.

"I guess it is. I didn't know that we have that feature on our phone. So, you could talk to the new girl at the same time," Mom said and headed downstairs.

"New girl?" asked Jade.

"Yeah, there's a new girl named Faith. This was her first week," I explained.

"Is she nice?" wondered Marie.

"She's okay. It was funny. She and I wore almost the same exact outfit on twin day. You know, the tie-dye skirt and the peasant blouse."

"I love that outfit!" chorused Jade and Marie in stereo.

"She must be cool then," continued Jade.

"I guess so. She's my partner for the science fair too."

"Hey! Why don't you invite her Saturday?" asked Marie.

"Yeah!" agreed Jade. "Let's meet the new girl! Call her now so we can have a group chat!"

"Can't," I replied. "I don't have her number."

"Well, just ask her tomorrow then," said Jade.

I agreed that it was a good idea. Jade and Marie always had great ideas. Jade suggested that we go apple picking Saturday morning and then make the caramel apples in the afternoon. Marie was allergic to milk, so she asked if we could make some candy apples too. Why not? It all sounded excellent to me. Their ideas got me thinking too. We could also dip the apples in chocolate. Oh! Chocolate-covered apples with sprinkles, or nuts, or maybe coconut! I loved food as much as I loved fall. Saturday was going to be awesome!

I couldn't wait to get to school the next day to invite Faith. I got there early so that I could talk to her before class started. Aimee and Amanda came in laughing and talking. Then Rachel and her sisters got there. I felt really awkward just standing there by myself, so I pretended to look for something in my locker.

I heard Kate and a boy chatting and turned to see that it was Kyle with her. Kate was giggling and flipping her hair as they were walking by.

Oh! It wasn't fair! I'd liked Kyle for like forever. Who did Kate think she was flirting with him? I looked in the locker mirror to see a sad face staring back. Why not me? Why was he talking to her and not me? My hair looked okay. I mean, it wasn't in a braid or anything, but it was brushed. Nope, no cream cheese on my mouth. I wasn't horrendous looking, was I? Maybe it was the freckles. That must have been it. No one ever liked freckles.

As I was staring into the mirror, I felt a tap on my shoulder. It was Faith.

"Hi, Lacy!" she said.

"Oh, hi!" I responded. "Hey! I want to ask you something."

"What is it?"

Before I could answer, the bell rang for class. No more talking until English was over. Mrs. Hart was really strict. I could see Faith looking over at me though with a worried expression on her face.

We read some more of *To Kill a Mockingbird* together, and then Mrs. Hart gave us worksheets about the chapter. The hour dragged on until I felt somebody poke me in the back. It was Kate, trying to give me a note. I really didn't want to take it from her. I mean, I didn't want another Amazon warrior note or a picture of a bloody knife like Marie had gotten last year. Mrs. Strickland hadn't wanted to believe the other girls were bullying Marie, but I knew better. It wasn't just that they gave her that horrible drawing and called her mean names like Chucky from the horror movie when the teachers weren't around; it was more subtle than that. They never made her feel welcome, and they always made sure she wasn't included. Whenever she would walk in the room, they would stop talking and move away to the other side. Then, at lunch, there was never enough room for her at their table. At gym, she was always the last girl to be chosen for teams. I still remembered the time the group wanted to surprise Mrs. Hart by covering her desk with sticky notes they had written. They had asked Mrs. Strickland for some sticky notes and had passed some out to all the girls except Marie, Jade, and me. Marie felt dissed, so she took some sticky notes to join in the fun, but Rachel saw her and grabbed them away, yelling, "No! It was our idea, not yours!"

Marie was so mad and hurt. She wouldn't even sign the card the others asked us to sign later. "Why should I?" she had asked. "They just want us to get in trouble, too, if they do for messing with Mrs. Hart's desk."

Reluctantly, I took the note from Kate and opened it. I didn't recognize the meticulous handwriting. "What's up?"

I looked around the room, but everyone was busy with the worksheet.

Mrs. Hart looked up and saw me. "Do you need help, Lacy?" she asked.

I heard someone snicker as I shook my head no, my face turning pink. I looked back down at my work.

Five more minutes, and class would be over. Feeling someone staring at me, I looked around again. Faith mouthed something. What was she trying to tell me? I never was good at reading lips. She tried again, exaggerating so I could see better. Nope, I had no idea what she was saying. I made what I hoped was an "I'm sorry" face and shrugged my shoulders.

As I turned back to my work, I noticed a shadow across my desk. Oh no! Mrs. Hart was standing right in front of me.

"Lacy, are you having problems with this assignment?" she asked with a stern voice.

"No, Mrs. Hart," I said.

"Good! I suggest you finish quickly. Class is almost over."

Now everyone was staring at me. Even though there were only two minutes left, it felt like forever until the bell rang. I grabbed my things to go. I didn't feel like talking to anyone. All the other girls were glancing over at me whispering. I rushed to get to my locker.

"Wait up! Wait a minute!" I heard a voice behind me, but no one ever talked to me, so whoever it was must have been yelling to somebody else. "Lacy!"

I stopped short and turned around. Faith was making her way through the crowded hallway. "Lacy, why didn't you answer my note?" she asked.

"Oh. I…" I trailed off.

"You didn't finish what you were saying before English class," Faith opined.

I just gave her a blank stare.

Impatiently, Faith continued, "You said you had something to ask me."

"Oh! It's not a big deal. My mom is in charge of the snack table for the fall festival this year. I'm going with a couple of friends Saturday to pick apples. We're going to make caramel apples for the snack table and thought that you might like to help too."

As I was explaining, Faith's expression changed from an anxious stare to an exuberant smile. "Cool! I'll have to check with my mom if anything is going on Saturday."

"Okay!" I smiled as I got my phone out. "What's your number? I'll text you the deets."

Before I knew it, it was Saturday morning, and for a change, I was waking Mom up. "Rise and shine and give God the glory, glory," I sang. "Time to get up and go pick apples, Mom!"

She looked at me skeptically and asked, "What time is it?"

"Seven o'clock! Let's go! We said we'd pick everyone up by eight."

So, Mom slowly got up and got some coffee, and we were on the road forty-five minutes later.

We picked up Jade first, then Marie.

"Hey! What did that sign say?" asked Marie.

"Hee, hee! Forget love. I'd rather fall in chocolate!" I replied. "That sounds about right. I love chocolate!"

"Too funny!" said Jade through giggles. "Maybe you should dip Kyle in chocolate instead of the apples."

I could feel my face start to turn red, and Jade was laughing so hard she snorted.

"You snorted!" cried Marie, and then we were all laughing so hard that our sides hurt, and I even snorted once or twice too.

Going to the orchard was always so much fun. Mom had been taking Dakota and me apple picking since, well, forever. Before I was even old enough to walk, she used to carry me on her back, and I would point to the biggest and reddest apples I saw. When I got a bit bigger, I would ride on Dad's shoulders and pick the best apples off of the tops of the trees where no one else could reach.

Mr. Parsons, the owner of the orchard, would always welcome us with a warm, friendly smile. "G'day, folks!" he would say, grinning from ear to ear. Then he would bow low to the ground, taking off his straw hat in a grand, dramatic gesture, asking, "And who are these two lovely young ladies that you have with you today?" Dakota and I would smile and giggle to be called "young ladies." Yup, Mr. Parsons always made us feel welcome, like family. In fact, he kind of reminded me of Grandpa Joe, always happy and smiling.

As we pulled into the parking lot, I could see Mr. Parsons over by his tractor. He looked just like I remembered him in his blue overalls and straw hat. He waved when he saw us and headed over to say hello. "Well, hello, ladies. Good to see you again. I hadn't seen you yet this year and was beginnin' to wonder if something was wrong."

Mom reassured him that we were all fine and added that Dakota was in her first year of college.

Mr. Parsons gave a long, low whistle.

"Is that right?" he said, shaking his head in disbelief. "Little Dakota has gone and grown up on us! Well, I guess we are all getting older." As he said this, I noticed his smile start to fade and the glimmer in his eyes dim just a bit.

He looked toward the orchard then and told us that the Red Delicious, MacIntosh, Macoun, and Empire varieties were at their peak right then.

We could also pick Gala, Granny Smith, and Rome if we liked. Actually, any row with an orange cone next to it was fine.

I started toward the rows of apples when I heard Jade suddenly yell out, "I bet I can get there first!" as she streaked past me. Then the three of us ran down the path toward the trees.

In the distance, I heard Mr. Parsons call out, "Remember that you can each taste test one apple while you're picking!"

It was a glorious morning. The sun shone brightly on us in the cool, crisp air. There were rows upon rows of apple trees. It was late in the apple-picking season though, so practically all of the apples that had been within arm's reach had already been harvested.

Jade was the tallest of the three of us, so she was able to reach more apples.

Marie, who was the shortest, kept trying to jump up and pull apples off of the higher branches, without much success. She looked like a little jackrabbit hopping up and down.

"I know!" I said. "You can ride on my shoulders, and we can get the best apples at the top that nobody could reach."

"Awesome idea, Lacy!" she said as she clambered onto my back.

It was really easy to carry Marie. She was so light.

Before we knew it, her bag was full of perfect, unblemished apples. Not a bruise in the bunch.

"You know, I can see the whole orchard from up here. Hey! I think that's Kyle and Tim over there. They look like they're with a girl!" Marie exclaimed.

What? I could feel my heart start to race. *No way!* I thought. There was no way I wanted to see Kyle there, then. Since it was a Saturday, and we were only going apple picking, I hadn't bothered picking out something nice to wear. I had put on my ratty old jeans and the lame pink sweatshirt with the kitten on it that Grandma had given me the year before.

"Yup," said Marie. "They are coming this way. Hi, Kyle! Hi, Tim!"

"Be quiet!" I hissed at her. "I don't want them to see us!" I said in what I hoped was a loud whisper so that she heard but the boys didn't.

I hadn't even brushed my hair or my teeth! I absolutely did not want to see Kyle looking like that.

"But I thought you liked Kyle," squealed Marie as I started running through the rows of apple trees with her clinging to me.

"Wait! Where are you going?" yelled Jade as she saw us bounding through the trees.

I didn't stop to answer her. I just wanted to get out of there, fast.

"Marie, which way should I go? Where is the parking lot?" I asked frantically.

"But we're not finished picking apples," she whined.

Oh, yes we were! At that moment, I didn't care how many apples we had. We were leaving. I sped up. The car had to be to the left, I reasoned. I turned the corner, but there were just more trees. I went up a little farther, then turned left again. Marie was getting heavy, her heels were digging into my sides, and the bag of apples kept banging wildly against my shoulder. My legs were burning and shaking from the physical effort. I needed to get to the car! I decided to turn right and find my way back to the main pathway.

"Lacy, slow down!" screamed Marie. "I can't hold on!"

Suddenly, I couldn't see anything. In her desperation to not fall off of my shoulders, Marie had clasped her hand over my eyes! I kept running in darkness for what felt like forever, but it was really only a minute or two until my foot got caught on the roots of a tree. Then we were flying through the air—me, Marie, and our huge bag of perfect apples. *Thunk!*

What in the world? I had hit something solid, but it wasn't a tree because I had knocked it over. Marie had fallen off of my shoulders, and I could see now, but I wished I couldn't. There was Kyle on the ground underneath me. He was looking up at me with a dazed expression on his face. Marie was a couple of feet away, and Tim was helping her up. Apples were everywhere. I was so stunned that all I could do was stare. Out of the corner of my eye, I could see Faith and Caleb trying not to laugh. There I was in Mr. Parson's apple orchard, sitting on top of my crush, looking like an idiot with Medusa hair. Great!

I heard some leaves rustling and then a click and a quick flash.

"I can't wait to show everybody at school!" chortled Alyssa.

"Just upload it today," said Rachel. "It's so funny. Why wait?"

What! Alyssa and Rachel were at the orchard too! No way! Worse yet, Alyssa took a picture! Now everyone would see me in my loser outfit squashing Kyle! I was so embarrassed I thought I would die right there.

"Nice of you to drop in." Kyle grinned as he stared up at me.

"S-s-s-sorry," I stammered, trying to get up, although my legs felt like jelly.

I had just managed to stand when I felt the world spin and my legs give way again. So there I was, sitting on poor Kyle, who had just sat upright.

"I must make a great cushion!" Kyle laughed.

I could feel my face turn crimson, redder than the reddest Red Delicious apple.

"Seriously though, are you okay?" he asked, a concerned expression on his face.

"Okay," I repeated slowly. "Okay, yes, yes," I said, sounding confused. Aargh! Why couldn't I just talk to him? Why in the world did I have to slam into him? *He must think I'm some sort of a weirdo!*

"Lacy! Are you all right?" It was Mom and Jade who had just rounded the corner onto the main pathway.

"Fine, Mom. I'm fine," I said, my voice trailing off.

Jade helped me up off of Kyle, her eyes wide as she realized what had just happened. Then she started to giggle, which turned into gales of laughter as Mom asked me who my friend was and was he okay.

Before I knew what was happening, we were all picking up the apples—Kyle, Tim, Jade, Marie, Faith, Caleb, Mom, and I—and everyone was smiling and talking at once. I introduced Faith and Caleb to Jade, Marie, and my mom.

Faith apologized for being late to meet us and explained that she had to wait for her brother, Caleb, to give her a ride. Since Faith couldn't find us in the orchard, she and Caleb decided to hang with Kyle and Tim when they saw them.

I overheard Marie telling Tim how we planned to make tons of caramel and candy apples that afternoon for the festival. I noticed Tim's face light up at the mention of caramel apples. I had known Tim for what seemed like forever. He went to my school and also to the same church as us. Sure enough, Tim was saying how much he loved caramel apples and how he and Kyle were in charge of decorations for the festival the next day.

Everyone was smiling, but I still felt awkward. I couldn't talk to Kyle even though I thought I saw him glance over at me once or twice. He must have been thinking what an absolute dork I was. I just wanted to finish picking up the apples and leave.

"You and Kyle could help us make the caramel apples, and we could help you guys with the decorations," Marie said gleefully. *Marie didn't just say that, did she? Did she really just invite Kyle and Tim over to my house?*

"What a wonderful idea! Don't you think so, Lacy?" asked Mom.

I couldn't believe it! I wanted to become invisible, but instead I tried to smile and just nodded in agreement.

The guys said they had to go buy supplies first, so we decided that they would come over after lunch, at about one o'clock.

We took all of our bags of apples and headed to the farm store to pay. Alyssa and Rachel were there picking out pies for the pie-eating contest the next day.

"Oh hi, Jade!" said Alyssa as she brushed past me.

Mom gave me a quizzical look. "Jade?"

"Whatever," I said. "Everybody always gets us mixed up."

It was true. All the adults, especially teachers, always confused me

46

with Jade. Maybe it was because we both had long brown hair. Maybe it was because we were almost the same height. Maybe it was just because we'd been inseparable since the fourth grade. Well, we *were* inseparable, I'd thought. I kind of hoped, though, that the other kids in my class at least knew my name. I mean, I'd known Alyssa since kindergarten too!

Feeling dissed, I walked over to the car and sank into the back seat. Jade and Marie piled into the car next to me.

"What's wrong, Lacy?" asked Marie. "Aren't you feeling okay?"

I didn't say anything and just looked down at the floor.

Jade looked over and asked sarcastically, "Aw, did you bruise your bum when you fell on Kyle twice?"

Hurt, I turned to glare at Jade but then started laughing when I saw the smirk on her face.

"Goof!" I exclaimed as I elbowed her in the ribs.

"Ha! Ha!" she laughed. "You looked so funny sitting there on Kyle!"

"Yeah," chimed in Marie. "The look on your face was priceless."

"And how about you?" I asked. "You landed on Tim!"

"Yeah, I did," she replied a bit dreamily.

"So, why should you be upset?" continued Jade. "You finally got to be close to your crush. Oh, Kyle!" She sighed as she raised the back of her hand to her forehead in a dramatic gesture.

"True," I retorted, turning red, "but he didn't seem too thrilled about it. Besides, I was running away from him because … well … well … Just look at my stupid outfit!"

Just then, Mom got in the car. "Your outfit? What do you mean? There's nothing wrong with what you're wearing. Grandma got you that sweatshirt for Christmas," she said.

I rolled my eyes and looked at my two best buds, who nodded sympathetically.

"Yeah, you should probably change when you get home," offered Marie.

"Why don't you wear the jeans and the cute sweater that I got you for your birthday?" suggested Jade.

As soon as we got back to the house, I quickly showered and put on the jeans and the purple sweater Jade had given me.

"You have such pretty hair," Marie commented. "I'll braid it for you."

"Okay!" I agreed. "With my luck, it'll wind up in the caramel if I don't let you."

Since we expected a fairly large turnout at the fall festival, we decided that we should make at least fifty apples. I loved Gala apples, but Jade insisted that we should get MacIntosh, something about that variety being traditional for caramel apples. Of course, Marie hadn't agreed with either of us and said that Red Delicious were best for making candy apples. In the end, we decided that our customers were probably like us and would all want something different, so we compromised and got some of each. Mom also got some Granny Smith for those who preferred a crisp, tart apple.

Before I knew it, it was one o'clock. Kyle, Tim, Caleb, and Faith were supposed to be there by then. Oh, well! They might arrive any minute. We may as well get things set up to make the caramel apples.

I started getting the popsicle sticks, the plastic wrap, and the toppings out on the kitchen table.

It was 1:30 p.m. when the phone rang. It was Tim. Was it okay if his brother, David, came too?

"No problem," I said. Well, why not? It was almost starting to look like a party!

Faith and Caleb showed up five minutes later. I showed them our apple-making operation, and we got to work.

I started to wonder if Tim and Kyle were really coming. Every minute or so, I couldn't help but look over at the clock. Jade caught me checking the time and looked at me sympathetically.

Fifteen minutes later, there was a loud knock at the door. I jumped up to go answer it, hoping that Kyle had finally arrived, but when I flung the door open, only Tim and David were standing on the front stoop. My heart sinking, I looked behind them for Kyle, who was nowhere to be seen.

"Where's Kyle?" I asked, trying to sound like I didn't care.

"Oh! His mom said he had to finish some chores around the house first," answered Tim as he walked in.

Whew! I thought. I'd be disappointed if he didn't come.

We were trying to decide how many of each kind of apple to make when the doorbell rang again. I ran to open it, but before I got there, I checked my hair in the hall mirror. Marie was right; my hair was pretty. I opened the door, and to my surprise, it was a pizza-delivery guy.

"Two cheese and two pepperoni pizzas!" he bellowed.

"What?"

I was about to tell him there was some mistake when Kyle came up behind him, saying, "Perfect timing!" and handed him the money for the pizzas.

Kyle smiled broadly and said, "Lacy, I hope you don't mind. I haven't eaten lunch yet, and I know that Tim and Dave haven't either." Then he took the pizzas and sauntered into the house.

Dumbfounded, I stood there a minute before joining the party.

"Awesome! You're here with the pizza!" commented Tim. "I'm really hungry. I haven't eaten since breakfast."

Marie and I exchanged a surprised glance as the boys began devouring the pizzas.

After a few minutes, Kyle looked up and said, "Oh, did you want some? There's still some left."

In a matter of only maybe fifteen minutes, the three boys had already eaten two whole pizzas. The girls stared in disbelief, but Caleb didn't wait another second, exclaiming, "Thanks!" as he scooped up a piece of pepperoni.

Then Jade spoke up. "Well, I'd like some. How about you, Lacy? Do you want to share a piece with me?"

I loved pizza, especially pepperoni, but the oil always made me break out, so I was glad that she wanted to share.

"Sure thing!" I answered. "I'll get us a plate."

Caleb grabbed a paper towel to catch the grease that was dripping off of his pizza.

Marie made a face and decided that she would stick with the hummus and pita chips Mom had put on the table for a snack.

We set up assembly lines to make the apples. Jade would wash them. David would dry them with a paper towel. Tim said he would place the popsicle sticks in each apple. Caleb would heat the candy to put on the apples, and Faith would dip them in the candy. Marie volunteered to dip the apples in the caramel since she had made them before. That left Kyle and me to decorate them how we liked with coconut, nuts, mini chocolate chips, or sprinkles.

Everything was going brilliantly! Marie was really good at swirling the apple in the caramel so that the whole apple was covered. I was determined to make the apples look amazing, so I was taking my time dipping them in the coconut and placing the chocolate chips on them when I suddenly heard Marie scolding Tim.

"What is this? You impaled this poor apple! It won't stay on the stick!" Marie said.

"What do you mean?" Tim protested. "I just put the stick into it."

"Well, you don't have to stab it so hard! There's no way I can dip this in the caramel now."

"Look, it's not my fault. The apples are hard. I have to push really hard to get the stick into the apple."

Then I turned to see Marie holding an apple on a popsicle stick, except the apple didn't stay on it firmly placed. It spun around like a top.

Marie had an aggravated look on her face when she said, "No, it can't be like this. Don't stab anymore of the apples, okay?"

In response, Tim said, "There's nothing wrong with it. Let me do it. You just don't know what you're doing."

As he was saying this, he grabbed the apple away from her and went to dip it in the caramel. Plop! The apple fell off of the stick and into the hot caramel with a major *kersplosh*.

"Ow! Ow! It burns!" he yelled as the steaming caramel splashed his hands and face.

"Fast! Go rinse it off with cold water!" I yelled.

Tim ran into the bathroom, and Marie, looking worried, hurried over to help him wipe off his face. Tim quickly threw cold water onto his face with his hands, and Marie took the towel and gently patted his face dry.

"None of it got in your eyes, did it?" she asked.

"No," he answered. "Hey! I'm sorry I acted that way. I guess you were right," he said sheepishly.

"No problem," she said. "I burned my hand the first time I made caramel apples too."

I was watching them smiling at each other when I felt somebody poke me in the ribs.

"Hey, slacker! I've made five more apples than you. Get to work!" It was Kyle teasing me. "You're not Picasso, you know. Just dip the apples in the sprinkles and move on!"

It was true. Kyle had done more apples than I had, but my apple did look amazing. I looked over at Kyle's apples. One was halfway covered with coconut. Another one had three chocolate chips on it. A third one only had nuts at the very top and nothing else.

Are you kidding? I thought. *No one is going to want to buy those!*

"Uh, Kyle, you call those decorated?" I asked.

"Yeah, I've done more than you. Just look," he answered smugly.

"Yeah, unfortunately, I did look. Would you buy any of those?" I asked, pointing.

"Of course. Why not?" he asked defensively.

I just shook my head. No way. No way would anyone I know buy those apples.

Just then, Jade came over to see how things were going. "Wow, Lacy! Your apple looks delicious. We could probably get four dollars for that one."

"How about mine?" asked Kyle hopefully.

Jade turned to look at the apples. "Oh, I don't know." She hesitated. "Maybe we could get one dollar each."

"Only a dollar!" Kyle retorted, insulted. "Why is Lacy's apple worth so much more?"

Hearing the commotion, Tim strolled over.

"Tim, what do you think? My apples are awesome, right? You'd pay three or four dollars for one."

Tim started to laugh and clapped his hand on Kyle's shoulder.

"Man, you're so funny. We're making caramel apples, not playing Mr. Potato Head. Maybe Lacy will help you," he said.

I looked over at Kyle, expecting to see him fuming over being the butt of the joke, but instead he was watching me with a slightly hurt expression in his big blue eyes and a hopeful look on his face.

"Hey, Lacy! How do you make your apples look so amazing?" Kyle asked.

"You want me to help you?" I replied.

He nodded, so I scooted over next to him.

"First, you have to envision what you want it to look like. You know, a sparkling brilliant white, like a new fallen snow. Then you take the apple and roll it in the coconut until it's covered," I explained.

Kyle picked up an apple and hurriedly passed it through the dish of coconut. There was some coconut on it, but it hardly looked amazing. He held it up to show me.

"Uh, no, not quite. Like this!" I said and gently took his hand holding the apple. I guided his hand as the apple slowly rolled in the coconut, one, two, three times to make sure it was completely covered.

He held it up and smiled as he said, "Wow, Lacy! You really are a food artist. This looks so much better. When I first rolled it, it looked more like brown snow that had already been plowed, but this looks like a field of freshly fallen snow."

I could feel myself blushing at the compliment as Kyle moved his chair closer and said, "We make a great team. You'd better help me with the chocolate chips and the sprinkles too."

By four o'clock, we had made seventy-five apples, and yes, they almost looked too good to eat.

We asked the guys how they planned to decorate the multipurpose room for the fall festival. They said that the principal had told them to get some cornstalks and pumpkins. They had already put them in the room.

"I bet you made a couple of scarecrows too," said Marie.

"And scattered fallen autumn leaves of bright orange and glowing gold," added Jade.

Tim and Kyle looked at each other awkwardly. "Uh, Pastor Dave just said to get cornstalks and pumpkins," replied Tim, looking down.

"There's not even a cornucopia?" I asked.

"A what?" Kyle asked.

"You know, one of those horn-shaped basket things with the plastic fruit people put on their table for a decoration at Thanksgiving," I answered.

"Oh, yeah," said Kyle, still looking unsure.

"Sure! My mom must have a bajillion of them! Aunt Monica sends her a bouquet of flowers in one every year for a centerpiece to put on the dining room table," I said as I jumped up and went to the hall closet to get one. "See! One of these!"

"Oh, yeah! I know what you mean now," said Kyle. "Nah, we don't have any of those things. Wow! I guess it's gonna look pretty bad, huh, Tim?"

"Yeah, and it starts tomorrow, right after morning church service."

I looked over at Jade and Marie. "Well, we did say that we'd help you guys decorate, didn't we?"

"Yeah, that's right," agreed Marie.

"Besides," chimed in Jade, "we would still be making the apples if you hadn't helped us."

"Okay then, what do we do?" asked Kyle.

"Marie, why don't you and Tim go and get us a few more supplies at the craft store?" I suggested. "You know, paper in autumn colors, a few more cornstalks to make scarecrows, maybe some streamers …"

"Yup! We'll get some harvest-themed decorations, too, if they have any," said Marie as she and Tim grabbed their jackets to leave.

"David and Kyle, can you guys finish wrapping the apples and put them in the box to bring tomorrow?

"Jade, I need your help looking for the cornucopia that my mom has stashed all over the house. I'm sure we can find at least a dozen to bring tomorrow. Oh! And we should find some clothes to dress the scarecrows."

Jade and I started our search in the kitchen closet. Not one cornucopia. We headed to Mom's craft room and looked through the closet there. Success! We found a cornucopia. Now we had two. I decided we should check the attic next. It was so much fun, like a treasure hunt! We had just gotten upstairs and had begun rummaging through some old boxes when Jade called me over to where she was. She had found it, the motherlode, a huge bin filled to the top with cornucopia, plastic fruit, and fake squash. I bent down to pick it up, but of course it wouldn't budge. Then Jade tried, but again nothing happened.

"Oh no! How are we going to get it downstairs?" I wondered out loud.

"You could ask your boyfriend, Kyle, to carry it. He's strong. Have you seen his muscles?" said Jade, giggling.

"M-m-m-my boyfriend?" I asked, startled.

"Uh huh. I saw you two decorating the apples. 'Oh, Lacy, could you help me? You're such an artist,'" mimicked Jade with a twinkle in her eye.

"Jade, you really think so? You really think he likes me?"

"What? Are you blind, girl? Have you seen the way he looks at you?"

I could feel my face getting warm, but I didn't care. Suddenly, I felt as light as a feather. I wanted to jump up and down, to laugh, to sing. Kyle did like me. I grabbed Jade by the arm, and we spun around like crazy lunatics.

"Jade, he likes me! He likes me!" I cried, and we laughed and spun until we fell to the ground, our sides splitting.

Suddenly, I shushed Jade. The stairs creaked. What if it was Kyle? What if he had heard us? I looked over toward the stairwell.

Mom peeked her head in the door and asked, "Are you two okay? I thought the roof was collapsing there was so much noise."

"Oh, Mom! We're fine," I replied. "Can we use these cornucopia for the fall festival tomorrow?"

"Of course! I never knew what to do with all those anyway," Mom said cheerfully.

"Oh! Can we borrow some old clothes too to make scarecrows?" I asked.

"Sure! Just look up here in the bins until you find something you like."

Creak. Creak. Thump. Thump. Creak. Footsteps on the stairs. We all looked over at the stairway.

"Hello? Hello? Anybody up here?" It was Kyle.

"Yes! Up here! Up in the attic!" I called.

A minute later, Kyle's face was peering over the railing, looking at us. He entered the attic with David, Caleb, and Faith right behind him.

"We finished packing the apples, but then it seemed like you were gone forever, so we thought you might need our help," Kyle said, smiling brightly.

Jade glanced over at me with an "I told you so" look, but I just grinned and said, "Oh, sorry! I guess we got carried away in our search. We found the cornucopia, but now we have to look for clothes for the scarecrows. Do you want to help?"

Kyle and David nodded in agreement.

Mom told us not to make too big of a mess and announced that she would be in the kitchen cooking supper if we needed her.

The first bin of clothing had my old little-kid clothes in it. Jade picked out a yellow and white sun dress with dainty little daisies on the skirt portion.

"Isn't this adorable!" she squealed.

"Um, yeah. I wore that when I was like four," I said, grabbing it away from her.

"Oh, and look at this cute sweater!" she continued, pulling out a light pink cardigan with teddy bears on it.

I wanted to die of embarrassment. I took it and shoved it back into the bin, closing the lid with a loud *thunk*.

"Those are all too small. Nothing in there is going to work for making a scarecrow," I said sharply. I just hoped that Kyle didn't think I was some sort of a dork now.

"How about this?" I looked over to see Caleb with a fluffy, hot pink bathrobe with big white polka dots wrapped around him.

"Ha! Ha!" crowed Kyle. "It's just your style, Caleb! Now, all you need is a shower cap."

Jade and I moved over to where they were looking. I found a bin with some of my mom's old clothes.

"Oh, this is it! Look, everyone!" I called as I held up orange and yellow plaid bell-bottoms.

"Wow! Those are totally rad, man!" joked Jade.

Kyle just shook his head in disbelief.

"Why? What's wrong with them?" I laughed. "They're autumn colors and everything."

We kept finding funny clothes and laughing. The guys found some of Dad's old clothes too.

David spied Dad's old high school football helmet and tried it on. I wish we had a camera. The helmet was so big that David practically disappeared in it!

Then Kyle found Dad's old tux jacket and tried it on. Wow! I didn't think Kyle could look any cuter, but in that jacket, he looked hot! Maybe that's why Mom fell in love with Dad. I remember her telling me that they met at the spring cotillion. She went to an all-girls school, and he went to an all-boys high school, so usually the boys and girls didn't see each other. The schools always combined for this special-occasion banquet and formal dance though.

"Whoa! This is gorgeous!" I heard Faith exclaim.

Turning around, I saw that she had in fact found Mom's cotillion gown. It was a beautiful powder blue, like a clear blue sky. The fitted bodice had a sweetheart neckline and tiny white pearls that sparkled in the light. Layers of tulle cascaded from the waist of the dress.

"Lacy, go try it on!" urged Jade. "I want to see what it looks like on someone."

"Oh, no! I couldn't!" I stammered. "I mean … it probably won't fit me."

"Oh, come on!" encouraged David. "We've all tried on something but you. It's not fair!"

"Yeah, try it on!" said Kyle. "It's fun! Don't be a party pooper."

Resigned, I took the dress from Jade and headed down to my room to try it on.

"Wait! I'll come help you," called Jade.

As I slipped the dress on, I heard Jade gasp, "Oh! You look … You look beautiful, just like a princess!"

The dress fit perfectly. The bodice fit like a glove outlining my petite figure, and the cascades of tulle emphasized my slim waist. I could hardly believe my eyes. I looked pretty!

"You have to go back upstairs to show Kyle!" squealed Jade.

Suddenly, I felt very self-conscious. It would be weird to have him looking at me in that. No, I couldn't do it. I shook my head no. No way!

Before I could change back into my jeans, I heard voices: "Lacy? Jade? Kyle? Guys, where are you?"

Marie and Tim were back from the craft store.

"Hey! Come see what we got!"

I stepped out into the hall just as Kyle was walking down the attic stairs. He saw me as he was nearing the bottom. His eyes grew wide until they seemed to be two enormous pools of the brightest blue imaginable, and his smile transformed to a look of awe as he stared at me, his eyes glazing over.

Neither of us said anything. Our eyes locked on each other. It all happened within an instant but felt like an eternity—a wonderful, glorious eternity. I could feel myself getting warm as the color rushed to my cheeks.

Just then, Marie reached the landing to the second floor. "Lacy, come see what ..." She didn't finish her sentence as we all heard a loud *thump* and saw Kyle lying on the floor. He had been so spellbound that he had missed the last two steps and fallen in a heap.

"Oh no!" we all cried and ran over to help him up.

"I'm fine, really," he insisted as he picked himself up.

Seeing that Kyle would be okay, everyone turned to look at me.

"Hey! I didn't know that there was going to be a festival queen!" Marie commented.

"Yeah, Lacy! You are definitely the queen," said Kyle, smiling as he brushed himself off.

"Oh, we were just looking through the old clothes in the attic to give the scarecrow something to wear," I answered, blushing.

"Well, I hope you don't think that the scarecrow can wear my gown!" Mom had come to see what all the commotion was about.

"Oh no, Mom! We just saw it and ..." I said.

"That's okay, Lacy. Did I ever tell you that that was the dress I was wearing when I met your father?" A dreamy look came over her face. "He was so handsome in his tux. He saw me from across the room and came right over to ask me to dance."

None of us knew what to say and started fidgeting awkwardly until Jade saved the day. "It is a beautiful gown. I'm sure you looked gorgeous."

Everyone nodded in agreement.

"Why, thank you! Have you found what you need for the scarecrow?"

"We found some bell-bottoms in autumn colors," I said.

"Yes, you can use those. Most anything up there will be fine. Nothing fancy though, okay?"

We agreed.

I changed back into my regular clothes, and we continued to look through the bins of clothing. Eventually, we found exactly what we needed for two scarecrows, including overalls and a plaid flannel shirt.

The next day was the fall festival. All of us arrived early to church to help the boys finish decorating. We set the scarecrows on bales of hay on either side of the entrance. Then we hung streamers, arranged cornstalks, pumpkins, and cornucopia, and scattered autumn leaves around the auditorium. I have to say it looked fabulous when we were done.

After the church service, participants set up their table or game. There were crafts, simple carnival games, a contest to see who could eat a doughnut off the string the fastest, the snack table, and a pie-eating contest.

When we set up the snack table, the apples caught everybody's eye as they entered the room. They looked and smelled delicious! Before we knew it, we had sold almost every one.

Everyone looked pleased as they visited the festival that afternoon. The grown-ups enjoyed the crafts and snacks while the kids were entertained by the carnival games.

We had just sold the last apple when Kyle came over.

"Wow. You sold all of the apples," he said, grinning.

"Yup! It was no problem. Everybody wanted one," I answered, smiling. "It must be because of our awesome decorating skills."

"Of course!" he replied. "We make a great team."

Mom glanced over and smiled knowingly when he said that. I tried to act like I didn't notice.

"Hey! Since they're all sold, why don't we go check out the games, Lacy! If that's okay with you, Mrs. Devlin?" Kyle asked.

My mom looked up from what she was doing. "Yes?" she said. "Oh, go ahead, Lacy. You'll just have to help me clean up before we leave."

Kyle and I walked around for a few minutes. We tried a couple of the games with no luck. Then we came to the ring toss. The object of the game was to get three out of four of the rings on the bottles without knocking them over. If you could do that, you'd win a prize. There were balloons, stuffed animals, and kiddie jewelry to choose from.

I tried tossing the rings first. Nope. I wasn't even close.

"Aw, I stink at this!" I said dejectedly. "I wish I could do this. That stuffed puppy is really super cute!"

"Which one?" Kyle asked. "The brown one with white spots or the black one?"

"Both are cute, but the brown one is cuter," I answered.

Kyle called the person in charge of the game over and bought a turn. He took the rings and held them in his hand as if he was weighing them. Then he asked me to hold them for him. He took the first one, planted his feet shoulder width apart, crouched down so that he was about the same height as the bottles, and let the ring go. It glanced off of the bottle in the first row, bounced up, and landed on a bottle a couple of rows behind it.

"Hey! Good job!" I exclaimed.

"Nah. It was supposed to go on that first bottle," he answered, grimacing. "This next one will be better."

He reached for the second one, took a step back, and flicked his wrist. The ring glided easily onto one of the bottles in the first row.

"Wow!" I said, impressed.

"Nothing to it," he answered.

Taking the third ring, he stepped back and concentrated on the bottles. I watched the smooth motion of his arm as he was about to flick his wrist when there was a loud *bang*. A little boy started to scream and then cry because his balloon popped. Kyle's concentration was broken, and the ring sailed over and behind all of the bottles.

"Oh no!" I cried.

Kyle looked aggravated but just said, "That's okay. There's one ring left, isn't there?"

I handed him the last ring. I started to pray silently that he would be able to ring the last bottle. Then I felt silly for praying for something so insignificant, but we are supposed to be able to bring everything to the Lord in prayer, aren't we?

I opened my eyes just in time to see the ring leave his fingertips, but Kyle was off balance when he threw it because the ring wasn't flat as it moved through the air this time. It was spinning on its side. The ring hit one of the bottles in the second row and rolled around on top of the bottles. We watched, mesmerized, for what seemed like forever until it finally fell down onto one of the bottles.

"Woohoo!" called out Kyle. "Pick whichever one you want, Lacy!" he said, smiling from ear to ear.

"Really? I can choose? But you won it," I said nervously.

"You said you like the brown puppy, right?"

Before I knew what to say, Kyle had the stuffed animal and held it out to me.

I could feel my face flush as he took my hand and led me over to the doughnut-eating contest.

"Let's try this one, next!" he suggested. "I didn't have any lunch yet."

All the contestants lined up in front of the doughnuts. I chose my favorite, a chocolate glazed. Kyle stood in front a Boston cream.

"On your mark! Get set! Go!" yelled the carnival worker.

About five seconds later, I heard, "We have a winner!"

I looked over to see a very happy Kyle with his mouth and nose completely smeared with custard. I started to laugh and told him that someone should take his picture. He laughed, too, and pulled me toward the photo booth.

I couldn't believe it! Here I sat, about to have my picture taken with my crush! We were so close that I could smell his cologne. I was so happy that I couldn't stop giggling, and my head was spinning.

He put the money in the machine and closed the curtain to take the picture. The first time the camera went off, we just sat there, smiling. The second time, I held up the stuffed animal so it would be in the picture too. The third time, I turned to look at Kyle, and we both made a funny face. He looked especially funny with the big blob of custard on the tip of his nose. I reached up to wipe it off of his face when the flash went off for the last time. Kyle wiped his face as we waited outside the booth for the strip of pictures. Finally, it came out of the machine, and he could see how he had looked.

"Wow! I guess I really enjoyed that doughnut!" He laughed.

"Yup! Oh, look! The last picture looks so bad! People will think that I was trying to slap you!" I said.

"Oh, yeah! It does kind of look like that, doesn't it?" he answered and then started pretending that I had hit him.

"Lacy! Ow! Why did you hit me? Ow! My nose!"

"Stop!" I cried, starting to laugh. "Everybody is looking at us!"

And they were. Alyssa and Rachel were turned in our direction, talking, and Rachel was pointing.

"Okay! Okay!" he said. Then he tore the picture strip down the middle so that we would each have a copy of the pictures.

We noticed then that the festival was almost all packed away.

"Oh! I'm supposed to help Mom clean up," I said.

"Yeah! I have to help Tim put the decorations away," Kyle said. "I'll talk to you later."

When I went back over to the snack table, I could see Mom smiling.

"Looks like you had fun. What are you going to name the puppy?" she asked.

I grinned. "Yeah, I don't know what I'll name him yet," I answered.

I texted Jade as soon as I got in the car. I couldn't wait to tell her what happened at the festival after she'd left. Of course, her response was "I told you so."

Then she asked me what I was going to name the stuffed animal. I told her I was thinking of naming it Choco or Sprinkles.

"No way! You should totally call him Kyle!"

How corny is that, I thought. I couldn't name it Kyle.

"Nope, too corny," I replied.

Jade texted back, "Seriously! He was so sweet to get it for you!"

I thought about it some more. I mean, I did want to remember the fun day we had together, but naming it Kyle? No.

"How about Donut?" I texted.

"Ha, ha! Good one," came the reply.

So, Donut it was. I loved Donut. He was sweet and soft and cuddly.

Bam! Bam! Bam! It was Monday morning, and my alarm clock was going off. This time, though, I hopped out of bed straightaway. If I got there early, maybe I'd have a few minutes to talk to Kyle before class started. I got dressed, grabbed my books and a granola bar, and we were off.

I arrived five minutes before the warning bell.

Great! I thought. *Kyle and I will have a chance to chat.*

I strolled in, expecting to find him at his or Tim's locker. I was surprised to see him casually leaning against Faith's locker, deep in conversation with her. Surprised, confused, and a little hurt, I hurried to the restroom before they could see me. They looked so happy, laughing and talking together. Why was he flirting with her?

Tears started to sting my eyes. I felt like a dope, a giant idiot, to think that Kyle liked me and was going to be my boyfriend. But why? We had had such an awesome time together at the fall festival. I had Donut and a picture to prove it. What had happened? Did I say something stupid so that he didn't like me anymore? I wracked my brain until the bell to go to class rang.

On my way, I brushed past Kyle, who was saying, "Hi, Lacy!" but I couldn't look at him. How fake was he anyway? I used to think he was sweet.

We were still reading *To Kill a Mockingbird* in English class. Mrs. Hart was talking about judging others and jumping to conclusions. She was asking us to think of times in our lives when that had happened to us or we had misunderstood a person or a situation. I could feel everybody in the room shift uncomfortably in their seat. I quickly looked around the room. Although Mrs. Hart was asking us a question, most of the girls were looking down at their book or notebook or fiddling with their pen. No one would look at her. Rachel felt my stare and glared over her book at me until I turned away.

Mrs. Hart had paused to wait for a response, but getting none, she continued, "We all have misunderstandings sometimes. Some are small and insignificant, and others can be large or turn into a bigger problem. Just recently, I brought a cake in to share with the other teachers. Everyone took a piece and thanked me, except for one person. If you were me, what would you think? What would you say or do?"

Aimee raised her hand. "Maybe that person doesn't like cake," she suggested.

"Or maybe they are on a diet?" offered Rachel.

"Did everyone know that they could have a piece?" asked Kate.

"Yes, everyone knew. I had even put a little sign in front of the cake, saying Free Cake," answered Mrs. Hart.

"Hmmm … so none of you think that I should be offended that this person didn't try my cake? I thought they must think I'm a terrible cook or they don't like me," Mrs. Hart continued.

"No way!" Alyssa blurted out. "I mean, everybody loves you."

The class nodded its agreement.

"Well, thank you, Aly! However, that isn't always the case, and adults sometimes have difficult relationships too. Actually, I did feel badly that this person did not want any of my cake. Should I have taken it personally? No. As you girls pointed out, there are plenty of other reasons why the person possibly didn't want any cake that had nothing to do with me."

"That's right," said Laura. "The person might be allergic to one of the ingredients in the cake. My brother is allergic to dairy."

Everybody started to talk at once then, mentioning someone they personally know with food allergies.

"Okay! Okay!" Mrs. Hart said after a moment. "So, do you think that I was wrong for being upset?"

Amanda raised her hand.

"Yeah, you were jumping to conclusions," she said. "Maybe the person just doesn't like chocolate cake."

"She never said it was chocolate," retorted Rachel.

"Well, you know what I mean," answered Amanda. "Maybe the person just doesn't like that kind of cake."

"So, what should I have done instead?" asked Mrs. Hart.

The room became silent.

Faith timidly raised her hand.

"You could ask the person why they didn't try a piece," she ventured.

All the other girls stared at her like she was from another planet then. Aimee started shaking her head from side to side. Laura frowned, and Rachel muttered, "No way."

Noting the girls' reactions, Mrs. Hart wanted to know why they wouldn't come straight out and ask the person.

"Awkward!" responded Kate, drawing out the syllables.

"You'd look like an idiot!" Alyssa nearly spat the words out.

I could see out of the corner of my eye that Faith looked a little hurt by their reaction to her comment. She sank lower into her chair and looked down at her paper.

Class was almost over, so Mrs. Hart told us to write a short paragraph for homework about a misunderstanding that we had that we could share with the class the next day.

I groaned inwardly as I wrote the assignment in my notebook. Now I would have to relive a horrible personal experience, write about it, and tell the whole class how stupid I was. Tomorrow would not be fun. The gang would love having something else to make fun of me for. What in the world was Mrs. Hart thinking?

The day dragged on. I managed to avoid seeing Kyle in the hallways between classes. That was a blessing because I really didn't know what to say or do if I did see him. Should I be friendly and pretend that I didn't see him flirting with Faith? Should I say something about it? But what would I say? Besides, it would have been awkward, like Kate had said, and I would look like a possessive witch. I mean, we weren't even dating, were we?

I got my books and made my way through the crowded hallway to science class. I got there just in time to hear Mrs. Strickland say that we should sit with our partner for the science fair project. She was going to hand back our project proposal so that we could work together on it.

Seriously? Why today? I absolutely did not want to have to talk to Faith. What kind of a friend would steal your crush away from you? I liked Faith and thought that maybe we could become besties like Jade and I were, but now? No way! Who did she think she was anyway? She thought that because she was new there, everyone would adore her?

I pushed my chair out from the desk, making a loud scraping noise as I moved to go sit with Faith. I could feel my jawline tighten as I grinded my teeth. Scowling, I plopped down in the desk beside her.

Mrs. Strickland came by with our proposal.

"Girls, you have some interesting project choices, but I think the question of which side of the body is dominant will work best as a partner project," she said as she placed it on the desk and then left us to discuss the project with each other.

I looked at Faith, who was looking over the proposal. I knew that I should say something, talk to her about the project, but I didn't want to. I kept seeing her laughing and smiling with Kyle, and I began to feel angry again.

She looked up at me with a wan, pasted-on smile. "We have our topic, so now what do we do?" she asked, her voice barely audible.

I tried to smile back.

"We have to research the topic and conduct experiments," I said.

"Oh!" she replied. "Does that mean we have to go to the library?"

"I suppose we really should." I sighed. "But we can find some articles on the internet too."

I didn't want to go to the library. It just felt like extra work.

"Tell you what! I'll start looking online tonight," I suggested. "You can go to the library, and we'll share the information."

Faith started to nod her head in agreement but stopped.

"I think we should go to the library together. I'm not very good at research," she admitted.

Oh, no! I thought. *It looks like I'm going to be stuck doing most of the project myself, even though I supposedly have a partner.*

I shot her an aggravated look.

"Well, okay. Can you go one day after school?" I asked.

Looking relieved, Faith said that she would check with her mom.

There was still class time left, and we could hear the others discussing their projects. Rachel and Alyssa were going to test different nail polishes to see which one lasted longer. Kate and Aimee were going to find out the best method of keeping food fresh for the longest time. Laura and Amanda were doing the crystal-growing experiment. I wasn't surprised. Someone always did the crystals project.

Mrs. Strickland came over to see how we were progressing on our project. She was concerned when she saw that we hadn't taken any notes. When we explained that we couldn't start the research in class, she nodded and encouraged us to begin thinking of how we were going to set up the experiment. How were we going to find out if it is better to be left-handed or right-handed?

"We could ask people," suggested Faith.

"Ask people what exactly?" I demanded. I didn't feel like being helpful.

"We could ask which hand they use the most," she offered.

"Okay, I guess ... but how many people should we ask?" I persisted. "I think we have to ask enough people to have a worthwhile sample. I know that that's not the scientific term, but you know what I mean, right?"

"Yeah, I think so," Faith replied. "If the sample is too small, the experiment won't really show us anything."

"Exactly!" I agreed, starting to smile for real. Maybe we could work together.

"We could start with our families ..."

"And people at school," I said, finishing her sentence. "Are we only going to ask one question, cause that's pretty lame, one question."

"You're right!" Faith concurred. "We need to have more questions ready. What should we ask?"

So, we spent the rest of class coming up with questions to ask our interviewees.

1. Which hand do you usually use to write?
2. Can you use either hand to write?
3. Which hand do your parents use when they write? (Maybe there is a pattern? We'll see!)
4. Do you play an instrument? Which one? (Because people who play piano might be more likely to be ambidextrous?)
5. When you walk, which foot do you step out on?
6. Do you play sports? Which one? Do you kick with your right or left foot? Do you bat righty or lefty?
7. Is the arm you write with stronger than the other one?

I was still wondering if lefties or righties were smarter. I mentioned this to Faith.

"That's funny! Why would one be smarter than the other?" she asked.

"I don't know. Maybe you're only smarter if you can use both sides equally?" I wondered.

Faith looked at me quizzically.

"How in the world would we test that?" she asked.

The bell signaling the end of class rang as she was asking the question, so I just shrugged my shoulders in response.

"Aaargh!" I screamed as I crumpled up another sheet of paper and hurled it toward the already overflowing wastepaper basket in my room. I had been trying to write the paragraph for Mrs. Hart's class for over an hour, and now there were at least a dozen balls of scrunched-up paper scattered on the floor. I hated the assignment! Why did we have to write about a misunderstanding? What did that have to do with class? We were reading *To Kill a Mockingbird*. What did our problems have to do with literature? I was so frustrated. Writing about a misunderstanding wouldn't have been so bad if I knew it wouldn't be shared with the class. But no! This was going to be shared, and I would have to be the one to stand up in front of everyone and tell them about it. I would have to let everyone know how stupid I was. Didn't Mrs. Hart know how difficult it was? Why did she want to humiliate us? I could feel my stomach tighten as I thought about being humiliated and mocked by the whole class. My throat got dry, and my eyes filled with tears.

Maybe I just wouldn't do it. How much would it hurt my grade to not do this one assignment? I got out the course syllabus to figure it out. Mrs. Hart didn't give us many writing assignments, so this would count as two homework grades. Then there was the presentation part of the assignment that would count as a quiz grade. I began to cry even harder. There was no way I could skip the assignment, especially since I had only gotten a B- on her vocabulary quiz the week before.

I was thinking about asking my grandparents if I could go live with them in Florida when I heard the phone ring.

Mom called out, "Lacy! It's Jade! Should I tell her that you're busy with homework?"

Jade would understand.

"No, no!" I croaked, my voice hoarse from crying. "I'm coming!"

I snatched a tissue to wipe my eyes and blow my nose before picking up the phone.

"Hey, Lacy!" came the bubbly voice on the other end.

"Hi," I mumbled.

"Hey! What's wrong?" asked Jade. "Are you sick? You sound like you're holding your nose."

"No." I sniffled. "Oh, Jade! It's awful!"

"What's awful?" she asked.

"I have to write about a misunderstanding for Mrs. Hart and present it in front of the class," I answered, starting to cry again.

"And ...?" said Jade.

"And what?" I sniffled.

"And what's the big deal?" she asked.

I couldn't believe it! Jade didn't understand! I was flabbergasted.

"I ... I ... I ... Jade, you know that they're all going to laugh at me!" Silence.

"Jade? Jade? Are you still there?"

"Yeah. I still don't see what the problem is. Just write about some dumb little misunderstanding with your mom or your sister."

I was ready to complain and say why I couldn't when I stopped and thought about what she had said. She was right! I didn't have to look stupid. I could pick something that was no big deal, something they had argued with their moms about too.

"Jade, you're amazing! If you were here, I would hug you!"

"Ta! No prob," she replied. "So, what else is going on? You can't seriously be crying over English homework."

So, for the next hour, I vented to Jade about seeing Kyle and Faith together.

She couldn't believe that Kyle would be mean after being so sweet just the day before.

"I know!" I whined. "That's what I don't understand! It's not like we had a fight or anything."

"So, what are you going to do, avoid him for the rest of your life? I think people will notice."

"I don't know!" I cried. "Tell me! What should I do?"

"You could act like you didn't see anything. You're sure they didn't see you, right?" Jade asked.

"No, they didn't see me, but you know I'm not a good actress. I can't pretend I'm happy when I'm not."

"Yeah, true," Jade conceded. "I guess you're just going to have to ask Kyle."

"What?" I couldn't ask him. "What would I say? Umm, 'I'm not sure that I'm your girlfriend, but why are you cheating on me with the new girl?'" I asked.

"Well, if that's how you feel ..." she responded.

"Jade!"

"Okay, you know I'm kidding. Just ask what they were talking about and see if he will tell you."

"Why does it matter what they were talking about?" I pouted. "He was flirting with her!"

"Do you know that for sure?" countered Jade.

Did I? It sure looked that way to me. But ... Could I have been wrong? This thought hadn't even occurred to me before. I was so busy being upset that I had accepted my perception of what I saw as the absolute truth.

"Lacy? You still there?" Jade said.

"Oh, yeah. Do you really think he wasn't flirting with her?" I asked.

"I wasn't there, but you should give him the benefit of the doubt."

"But I can't! I can't ask him! I'm afraid!"

"What do you mean?"

"I mean … I mean … What if he was? Then I'll look really stupid."

"Lacy, what if he wasn't and you lose out on a great relationship because you *thought* you saw something that you didn't?"

I started to cry again, tears streaming down my face.

"Lacy! Lacy! Stop crying!" commanded Jade. "Stop being a baby! You have to decide. Are you going to find out what they were talking about or not?"

I tried to stop crying, but I was hyperventilating.

"Lacy, calm down. Maybe if you can't ask Kyle, you could talk to Faith?" Jade continued.

I finally stopped shaking long enough to answer. "Maybe … I do feel kind of bad that I was a grouch with her today."

"Good! Talk to Faith tomorrow. Then call me. Lacy, I wish I could talk longer, but I really have to go. My dad is mad that I've been on the phone this long. Bye!"

I hung up the phone and wiped my eyes on my sleeve. *How I wish Dakota were here! She would be able to help me. I mean Jade was great, but Dakota would analyze the whole thing with me. She would know just what to say!*

I tossed and turned all night long, unable to sleep, wondering exactly what I should say to Faith, or Kyle, or both of them. The night seemed to last forever, like time wasn't progressing: 1:00 a.m., 2:00 a.m., 2:30 a.m., 2:45 a.m., 4:00 a.m.

Finally, though, it was time to get up and get ready for school. Even though it was morning, the sky was still dark as a light rain was falling. I felt my way over to the light switch, shuffling my feet along so I wouldn't trip on anything. Just as my toes hit something soft, I heard a whimper. Oh no! I'd kicked Sticky. She had stayed with me all night to comfort me. I bent down to pet Sticky, saying I was sorry.

I flicked on the light to see my tear-stained face, now with wrinkles added from crying into my pillow. Hopefully a hot shower and some light makeup would fix it.

The next thing I knew, Mom was yelling up the stairs to me. It was already time to leave, and I had just gotten dressed. Quickly, I put on some moisturizer, foundation, and a hint of blush and hurried downstairs. I would have to fix my hair on the way there.

As we pulled in, I could see Faith and her brother, Caleb, getting out of his car. I got my bag and hurried to catch up with them and walk in together.

As I got closer, I could hear Caleb telling Faith not to worry, that she knew she hadn't done anything wrong. Just as he finished saying that, Faith turned around and saw me.

I waved, but instead of waving back, she got a strained look on her face and walked faster toward the door away from me. Well, it looked like it would be difficult to talk with Faith about Kyle. Why didn't she want to talk to me? Was she mad because I was grouchy yesterday? Or was she trying to hide something?

I entered the foyer as the warning bell rang. As I hurried to my locker, I saw Kyle laughing with Caleb and Faith out of the corner of my eye. Unfortunately, I had to pass by them to get to English class. They all looked so happy, smiling and talking, until I went past. Then they all stopped and stared at me, cold like wax figures. What was going on? Why was everyone mad at me? Why didn't anyone like me? I fought the urge to cry. Crying in public definitely wasn't cool.

After beginning the class with prayer, Mrs. Hart asked for volunteers to present their paragraph about a misunderstanding.

Aimee raised her hand, and then Kate did. Both of them talked about a misunderstanding they had had with a sibling.

Rachel presented her paper next. She told us how she'd gotten into trouble with her mother because she had mistakenly hung up the phone when her grandmother had called. Everybody was smiling and laughing. It was a good story because Rachel had made it funny. Who knew that a misunderstanding could be funny?

Next, it was my turn. After talking with Jade the night before, I had decided to write about a misunderstanding Dakota and I had had. We both thought that it was the other person's turn to take Sticky for a walk, so we both assumed that Sticky had already gone outside. Well, that's what we thought until Sticky made a mess on Mom's favorite rug! Mom was furious, and we both had to clean it up. When I finished my story, all the girls were looking at me like I was covered in poop.

"That's disgusting!" Rachel said loudly.

Aimee and Amanda agreed, commenting, "Ew! Gross!"

Fortunately, Mrs. Hart shushed them.

"What a great example, Lacy! Thank you!" she said. "Lacy's story shows us what happens when we assume and don't communicate with each other. I'm sure that Lacy and her sister ask each other if the dog needs to go out since that incident."

I nodded yes. We definitely didn't want that to happen again!

It was Faith's turn to present her paragraph. We all turned to her expectantly, but Faith didn't seem like she wanted to stand in front of the class. Reluctantly, Faith took her place at the podium. She started speaking, but she was so quiet that no one could hear her. Mrs. Hart encouraged her to speak up, to project her voice as if she were cheering at a football game. Faith started again, louder this time but still barely audible. She looked stiff like a statue and stared at the floor instead of looking at us.

"Faith, dear, please look at your audience. This will make it easier for us to hear you also," prompted Mrs. Hart.

Finally, I could hear what Faith was saying.

"I came here, hoping to make new friends," she started again.

I could feel the girls in the room shift uncomfortably in their seats.

"My first day here was great. Everyone was so nice, especially Lacy. She was the first person to greet me and show me where class was."

I started to smile. That was true. We had even worn matching outfits without realizing it.

"My brother and I even helped Lacy and her friends prepare for the fall festival," Faith continued.

Now I was confused. I thought that the paragraph was supposed to be about a misunderstanding. Obviously, from the expression on Mrs. Hart's face, she was confused too.

"Why, that's wonderful, Faith, that you made a good friend so quickly!" interjected Mrs. Hart. "But the assignment was to discuss a misunderstanding."

Suddenly Faith's voice cracked, and she blurted out, "That's just it! I had a good friend until I ruined it by not realizing how nice she is! I listened to other people, mean girls, who said that she's boring and dumb. They made me think that she's weird and not worth hanging out with. I didn't understand that those girls were just being mean. They weren't trying to be my friend by putting someone else down. They were just being controlling, selfish brats. Now I don't blame Lacy if she doesn't want to be friends."

The room was completely silent.

I couldn't believe it! Faith had just outed the other girls in front of Mrs. Hart. I didn't know what to do. I couldn't look at Faith, who had rushed to her seat, and I was afraid to look around the room at the rest of them. I could already imagine the grimaces and scowls on their faces, especially Rachel's. It was obvious from her demeanor that she thought she was perfect. What I didn't know was how Mrs. Hart was going to react.

It felt like ages until Mrs. Hart said, "Faith brings up a good point."

The fidgeting and shuffling of feet that could be heard a moment earlier stopped as she started to speak, and again, quiet enveloped the room.

"Misunderstandings are not just not understanding what someone has said but also having the wrong idea or perception about someone or something. Let's think about this in terms of the novel. What do Jem and Scout first think about their neighbor Boo Radley? Does their opinion of him change?"

As Mrs. Hart was asking the question, the bell rang, and we all began to collect our things to move to the next class.

"Class, think about how Jem and Scout think about Boo Radley for tomorrow. We will discuss how people's perceptions can cause misunderstandings," Mrs. Hart instructed.

We all filed quickly out of the room, not listening to the assignment but instead thinking about what Faith had just said.

Rachel and Alyssa were talking together quietly and glancing maliciously over at Faith as they walked out the door.

Oh no! I thought. *What has Faith done to herself?*

When I reached the science class, the girls were huddled together in a circle. All of them were complaining and griping. Once in a while, one of them would glance back over her shoulder at Faith, who was already seated. Poor Faith! She was trying to act like she didn't notice that they were all talking about her, or at least that it was no big deal, but I could tell the way she ruffled through her bag nervously that their rude behavior bothered her. She didn't want to look at them and kept her eyes averted from the group.

I went over to sit next to her since we were working with our science fair partners.

So totally awkward! My mind was a jumble of conflicting thoughts and emotions. My tongue was tied in knots, and my stomach was no better. I knew I should say something, but what? I was still aggravated with Faith for stealing Kyle away from me. She had, hadn't she? It certainly looked that way from the way they were always talking and laughing together, and she had acted like she didn't want to talk to me. But how could I be mad at her when she had just defended me in front of the whole class?

I had to stop and let that sink in. Faith had stood up for me in a very public way. She had just told the gang that they were mean and wrong for making fun of me and excluding me. Faith was risking not being one of the popular girls to expose them for being bullies. Faith was being my friend. A real friend with integrity! Could I have been wrong about her and Kyle?

I looked over at Faith again. She was trying to act like everything was cool, like she had no problems and that it was a normal day, but her smile looked plastered to her face. It was a stiff, forced smile, and she didn't look at all relaxed sitting on the edge of her seat, tightly gripping her pen.

The bell rang, and class began. Mrs. Strickland was talking about the science fair. We were to hand in a list of our sources for the research paper next week, so we needed to start our research today. Therefore, we would spend the rest of the class at the school library, getting started.

I looked over at Faith as we all picked up our backpacks.

"Well, at least we can start looking for articles and maybe find a book or two. We'll still probably have to go to the public library though," I said.

Faith didn't answer; she only nodded her agreement.

Since we had the whole hour to work on research, Faith and I didn't hurry to the library. However, the rest of the girls moved quickly, almost racing there. As we rounded the corner to the library, I could see Rachel holding the door for the others. We were two steps from the door when the last of the group entered. Rachel smiled mischievously when she saw us, and just as Faith reached the door, she left, letting the door slam in Faith's face. Poor Faith! She stood there stunned for a second, then she looked like she might burst into tears.

"That was so mean!" I said. Then I added under my breath, "She's such a witch."

Faith looked over at me and said teasingly, "I heard that!" as she opened the door.

We walked in the library, laughing, glad to have someone else who understood.

Our happiness was short-lived, however, as we realized why the others had hurried to reach the library first. There were only six computers in the library, and they had made sure that they all had one to work on. We would have to research our topic the old-fashioned way, at least for now.

We headed over to the encyclopedias and found some info under *right dominance*. Scientists called it sidedness, laterality, handedness or left/right dominance. Right-handedness or dextrality meant that a person was more dexterous using their right hand for manual tasks. Most of the world's population fell into the category of right-handedness (90 percent)! Left-handedness or sinistrality meant that a person completed manual tasks better when using the left hand. Only about 10 percent of the population was considered left-handed.

I turned to Faith and stated the obvious. "So, if we use one side of our body more for writing, throwing or kicking a ball, or doing general tasks, that is our dominant side."

"Right, but what about people who use the left hand to throw and the right hand to write?" she asked.

I looked back at the encyclopedia, scanning the page.

"Look! Here it is," I said, pointing and then proceeded to read, "'Mixed-handedness is when people tend to perform different tasks better with different hands.'"

"How many people are mixed-handed?"

"It says here that about 5 to 6 percent are mixed-handed.— thought the number would be higher than that! I use both hands to do different things. Don't you?" I asked Faith.

"No, that sounds about right. I know that I'm not ambidextrous."

"Not ambidextrous, mixed-handed!"

"That's the same thing, isn't it?"

"Not according to the encyclopedia. Ambidextrous means that a person is equally good at using either hand to perform any task. This is rare. Only 1 percent or less are ambidextrous."

"Oh, well, I might be mixed-handed. I'm not sure. I usually do most things with my right hand."

Faith found another entry in a medical encyclopedia and called me over to show me what it said.

"Look! According to scientists, handedness is somehow connected to our brain because the brain tells the body what to do," she said.

"Cool!" I murmured, reading the entry. "The brain is cross wired. The left side of the brain controls the right side of the body and vice versa."

"Yeah, but it's not absolute," Faith said. "Look! It says that for lefties, both sides of the brain work together sometimes."

We read a little more to find out that language and fine motor skills, like tying your shoes and using a pen, were handled most of the time by the left side of the brain, no matter which hand you used.

"So, different parts of the brain are responsible for different functions," mused Faith. "I don't know how this is going to help us with our project though. How does this answer any of our questions?"

"Oh! We can use this as background info to write the research paper," I said. "Let's make a photocopy of these pages so that we don't forget what source we found it in. We do have to figure out an experiment though."

Faith nodded as we walked over to the copy machine.

After science, lunch was next. I decided to text Jade.

"IDK what to think of Faith. She stood up for me versus the gang. But she's always laughing with Kyle. So confused. Help!"

About a minute later, my phone started to vibrate. It was Jade texting me back. "She stood up for you? Wow! You'll have to call and tell me more."

I grabbed my lunch and went to the cafeteria, steeling myself for another lonely half hour. The gang went to sit in their usual spot. Faith had put her lunch down on the table like always and had gone to the counter to buy a bag of chips.

I was eating my lunch and reading when I heard a commotion. I looked over at the table of girls and saw that Faith wasn't sitting with them. She was standing to the side, an anguished expression on her face; anger, hurt, frustration, and humiliation mixed in a fierce swirl of emotion. I heard her demanding that the girls give her lunch back. However, the only responses were sly smiles and snickering. The girls carried on their conversations with one another as if Faith was not even there. Faith looked like she would burst into tears, punch them, or do both.

I could feel my stomach twist into a knot and sink like a rock. They were at it again, being mean. I could see Rachel and Alyssa smirking as they continued talking and ignored poor Faith.

I should do something. But what? If I went over, they would just ignore me too, like they always had. I couldn't leave Faith standing there alone though.

If Faith went to the teachers for help, it would be worse. The teachers would ask if the others had seen Faith's lunch. The girls would play innocent and deny knowing anything. The teacher would just shrug and ask, "Are you sure that you brought your lunch today?" Or "Did you check your locker?" Then the teacher might say, "Let's get you a peanut butter sandwich." They wouldn't confront the bullies and make them give back Faith's lunch though. They wouldn't reprimand their bad behavior. I glanced over again.

Faith was still standing there, shifting from foot to foot, clenching her fists and wiping her eyes. Suddenly, without even thinking about what I was doing, I jumped up and marched over to the table.

"Faith, it's okay. You can sit with me," I said as I put my arm around her shoulder.

"But my lunch," she said, sniffling.

"Do you like ham and cheese? You can have half of my sandwich."

She looked up at me gratefully and wiped a tear off of her cheek.

We sat there a minute, not knowing what to say. Silently, we ate the sandwich and her chips. Faith still looked upset but wasn't crying anymore.

"Thanks!" I said.

"Huh? Lacy, why are you thanking me? I should be thanking you," she answered, surprised.

"I need to thank you for standing up for me in English class," I said. "That took a lot of courage."

Faith's eyes began to tear up again.

"It makes me so mad that people act that way to each other!" she said with clenched teeth. "After all, we are supposed to be Christians, modeling ourselves after Jesus."

I nodded. It was disheartening.

The bell rang for the end of lunch, and everyone started to clean up and leave.

On her way out, Rachel passed by our table and carelessly dropped Faith's squashed lunch bag on our table.

"We just found your lunch. Amanda didn't know she was sitting on it. Sorry," said Rachel in that sticky sweet, sarcastic tone that meant she wasn't sorry at all.

I could feel Faith tense up again, so I put a gentle hand on her shoulder and whispered, "Ignore her."

Faith snatched her lunch bag and hurried to her locker without saying a word.

I sure would have a lot to tell Jade when I talked with her!

As soon as I got home, I phoned Jade and told her everything that had happened.

"So, now I really don't know what to think of Kyle and Faith!" I moaned. "What do you think?"

"Well, did you actually ask either of them?" Jade demanded.

"No! How could I ask Faith that after she was already upset!"

"Well, either you want to know or you don't," Jade stated matter-of-factly.

"Oh, come on! I thought you would help me," I complained. "You sound like my mom."

"Okay! Okay! I don't know. I mean, you say it looks like she and Kyle are acting like a couple. On the other hand, she definitely just stood up for you."

"I know, right?"

"She does know that you like Kyle, doesn't she? Maybe, if she doesn't know, she doesn't think anything of flirting with him."

"Doesn't know? Well … I really didn't tell anyone at school. I can't remember if I told her."

"She saw you and Kyle together at the fall festival though. You'd think after seeing you two together the other day that it would be obvious. She must have been jealous."

"She saw us together at the festival," I murmured, trying to remember. "You know, I think she left the festival before Kyle and I started hanging around together that day."

"Oh! Well, then! Maybe she doesn't know. But what is Kyle's excuse? He definitely knows."

"True. I'm still confused. Does he like me or her?"

"Yup! You're going to have to ask him."

"Oh, Jade! I can't!" I answered, a whine creeping into my voice.

"Like I said, Lacy, either you want to know or you don't. It's up to you."

I hung up the phone with shaking hands. I was going to ask Jade for help knowing exactly what to say to Kyle, but she had to go do her homework. What was I going to say to Kyle? I would just have to pray about it. Pray and ask the Lord for guidance and wisdom to know what to say and, more importantly, what not to say!

"Okay, class. What do Jem and Scout first think about their neighbor Boo Radley? Does their opinion of him change?" asked Mrs. Hart.

Nobody said anything for what seemed an eternity, and then Faith slowly raised her hand.

"They thought that Boo might be some kind of a monster at first. They were afraid of him," she said.

"Yes, that's true," agreed Mrs. Hart. "That's a good start. Aimee, do you have anything to add? What about you, Rachel?"

Aimee squirmed uncomfortably in her seat, and Rachel quickly looked down at her notebook.

Mrs. Hart cleared her throat and said, "Class, why were Jem and Scout afraid of Boo Radley?"

Why were they afraid of him? I wondered. He hadn't been mean to them. He didn't speak to them; they had never even seen him.

"Lacy, what do you think? Why were the children afraid of Boo?" Mrs. Hart asked, turning to look at me.

"I don't know. They never even saw him," I replied.

"That's right! They didn't see him. Excellent observation, Lacy!" Mrs. Hart exclaimed.

Then she asked, "Were any of you afraid of the dark when you were little?"

A few of the girls nodded yes.

"Well, why were you afraid?" the teacher prodded.

Kate raised her hand and said, "It was dark. I couldn't see anything."

Aimee agreed. "It was scary because I didn't know what was there! There could have been a monster in the closet!"

"So, what you're saying is that you were scared because you didn't know what was there or what could be there," added Mrs. Hart.

"Yeah, I guess," said Rachel. "The not knowing was creepy!"

"Okay, so do Jem and Scout know what Boo Radley looks like?" asked Mrs. Hart.

Then it sank in. Jem and Scout were scared because Boo's identity was a mystery. It was like he was in the dark. He never came out of his house. No one knew what he looked like, so everyone was free to imagine him any way they wanted.

"That's right, Faith! The children's fear was the fear of the unknown," said Mrs. Hart. "Often, the unknown is scarier than the known. But why is that?"

My hand shot up. "It's scarier because your imagination can get carried away," I said. "The unknown can be anything you imagine."

"Exactly!" concurred Mrs. Hart with a smile. "So, why do you think he is called Boo? Is that his real name?"

"Boo!" shouted Alyssa. "It's like at Halloween or when you're trying to scare someone, surprise them."

"So, even the character's name, or in this case nickname, shows that there is something scary or surprising about them," explained Mrs. Hart.

"But why isn't he just called Boo? Why attach the nickname to his last name, Radley?"

Just as Mrs. Hart finished the question, the bell rang to move to the next class.

"Please think about this question for tomorrow, class," she called as we filed out of the room.

Wow! I had never thought about character names before. I had always just accepted the names as a simple fact. I never thought it could mean something to the story. Why wasn't the character just called Boo? It was clear to everyone who Boo was. Why mention the last name? I was thinking about that as I walked to my locker. Obviously, I wasn't paying attention to anyone around me because I was surprised when I almost walked right into Caleb standing in front of my locker.

"Lacy," he said brusquely, "I have to talk to you."

"Me? Why?" I asked, surprised. "About what?"

"I can't tell you here. It's about Faith."

"Oh, okay …"

"I'll meet you here at the end of school today. Don't leave before we talk. Okay?"

"Okay …" I answered uneasily.

"Good!" he said with a sigh of relief as he hurried to get to his class.

Questions started swirling around my brain, trying to figure out what Caleb wanted to talk about. Did he know how the gang had been mean to his sister? Was he going to tell me that Faith liked Kyle so I should just butt out? Somehow, I really doubted that he wanted to tell me that Faith was glad I was her friend or how wonderful it was that we were science fair partners. Because I didn't know what he wanted to say, I just automatically suspected the worst.

I got to class just as Mr. Grimes was closing the door. I quickly took my seat and started to get my book out when I heard the rumble of Mr. Grimes's voice.

"Put all books and notebooks away. Test time!" he said.

Oh no! I had completely forgotten about the math test. I had meant to ask Dad for help before the test. Today definitely was not my day.

Thirty minutes later, I was only halfway through the exam. I could hear chairs scraping and feet shuffling as the other girls handed in their tests.

Why couldn't I be as good at math as Dakota? She always blazed right through math problems with seemingly no effort.

I kept working as fast as I could. The other girls were whispering now since they were done. Did I just hear my name? More whispers ... the name Faith and muffled laughter.

"Five minutes left!" boomed Mr. Grimes, making me jump.

Only two problems to go. I can do this! I thought, trying to convince myself. I hurried to finish, but it was difficult to concentrate. Half of my brain kept thinking about what I thought I overheard, and my ears were strained trying to eavesdrop on their conversation.

"Time's up!" called Mr. Grimes just as I wrote the last answer and the bell rang.

Caleb was standing by my locker at the end of school. "Hey, Lacy! You've got a few minutes to talk, right?" he asked.

"Sure!" I answered, trying to sound positive. It was so awkward. Caleb was two years older than me, and I hardly knew him. I mean the only times we'd ever spoken was when his sister, Faith, was there. Now he wanted to talk with me privately.

"Okay, here's the thing," he started, looking around to make sure no one else was listening. "You know that Faith and I just moved here, so everything is kind of new?"

"Uh huh." I nodded in agreement to let him know that I was listening as I got my books into my backpack.

"Faith would never say it, but she really misses her friends back home in Georgia," Caleb continued.

I smiled weakly, trying to look like I understood, which of course I did! I mean, Jade, duh!

Rachel and Alyssa came over to their lockers then, looking at us out of the corner of their eye and laughing like we were the funniest joke ever.

"You got all your stuff?" Caleb suddenly asked.

"Yeah, almost," I answered.

"I think we should walk," Caleb said, looking toward Rachel and Alyssa.

"Oh, yeah. I just need my math book," I said as I plunked it in my bag.

Caleb waited until we were a few steps away and then continued with a frown. "So, I think Faith might be having a hard time making friends."

Well, with the gang, I wasn't surprised. Faith was super nice, and knowing how they were acting the past couple of days, I could tell by her reaction that she wasn't exactly happy.

We were almost by the front door by then, and I was about to ask Caleb if Faith told him what happened in English class or at lunch the other day when I heard giggling. I looked up to see Faith standing against Kyle in the doorway, laughing hysterically. My stomach flipped, and I could feel my face fall to the floor. I tried to act like it was no big deal, before anyone noticed, but my smile felt forced. I knew if they looked in my eyes, they would see the words that I could not—would not—speak: "This definitely does not look like a poor, lonely girl who is having a hard time making friends!"

I had been feeling badly that the gang was mistreating Faith. I had felt a sense of camaraderie with her, a sort of kinship. Now, though, I was seething with anger as I again felt betrayed by the girl I had hoped would become my new best friend at school. What was she doing anyway? Why was she touching Kyle?

Caleb's voice interrupted my thoughts as he said, "Lacy, Faith found this in her locker yesterday." He took out a crumpled piece of paper and shoved it into the outer pouch of my bag. "Maybe you can recognize the handwriting. I'll talk to you about it later."

Then he called to Faith, "Come on! We gotta go! Mom will wonder where we are."

Faith grabbed her bag, smiled sweetly, waved to Kyle, and then they were gone.

I stood there in a daze, just watching. It was as if I was invisible to them, or I was at the theater watching a play, and they were the actors. Neither Faith nor Kyle even noticed that I was there.

Feeling like an unwanted outsider made me want to cry, but I decided that I wouldn't let them do that to me. I wasn't going to give them control over my emotions anymore. I just wouldn't think about it. So, I kept myself busy all afternoon and evening, playing with Sticky, helping Mom with supper, doing my homework. I even cleaned my room! It was working too. I was happily belting out one of my favorite songs when I absentmindedly reached over to my book bag and took out the crumpled paper that Caleb had hurriedly stuffed in there. I opened it up to reveal the word *loser* scrawled on it in black marker. Dripping from the letters in red ink were drops that looked like blood. Horrified, I immediately dropped it on the floor as if the piece of paper itself could somehow physically hurt me.

This is what Faith found in her locker? My stomach lurched then, and my heart was heavy. "Oh, no! It's happening all over again!" my brain screamed. "They're bullying Faith just like they bullied poor Marie!"

I picked up the paper reluctantly and looked at it again. No wonder Caleb was concerned, but what could I do? What could I tell him? I mean, I didn't really know who wrote the note. I only knew that they were mean to Marie last year too. I couldn't accuse anyone; then I would get in trouble. "Besides, why should I help Faith? She stole Kyle away from me," a little voice in the back of my mind reminded me.

The rest of the night, though, I couldn't keep from feeling sad and guilty. I wanted to text Jade to see what she thought, but I knew that she would already be asleep by then. I decided to text Dakota instead. She wouldn't mind.

"Hi sis. Have ? about bullying. Need yr advice."

I must have been really tired, though, because I fell asleep waiting for her answer.

The next thing I knew, I was at school, but I couldn't get in the building. I could see myself outside the doors, frustrated. I began knocking on the doors and peering in the windows, but they were all locked. Through the window, I could only see shadowy figures but couldn't distinguish who they were, and I couldn't get their attention. *Why won't anyone let me in!* Eventually, some of the figures became more distinct, and I noticed that they were girls my age. I pounded harder on the window, and then one of them turned around. It was Faith, and she was crying, an anguished look on her tear-streaked face. Then I noticed that the other girls were yelling at Faith. They began to encircle her and started shoving her from one to the other. I started pounding frantically at the door, screaming, "No, no, let me in, let me in!" and wondered, *Where are the principal and the teachers? Faith needs help!* I ran from window to window, trying to find somebody to help. Finally I saw the principal with Mrs. Strickland. They were talking, and the principal was waving something in his hand, showing it to Mrs. Strickland. What was it? What did he have? Suddenly the discussion became heated. They were obviously arguing as the principal slammed the paper down on a desk. It was the note Faith had gotten in her locker, but it was attached to a disciplinary sheet with the words *expelled* and *vandalism* on it in big red lettering. I tried to yell, to scream that it was all a misunderstanding, that Faith was not the vandal, but my voice would not work. No sound came out no matter how hard I tried. I was mute. Desperate, I tried to break the window, break the glass to get into the school, but my tiny fists just bounced off. Exhausted and ashamed for having not helped Faith earlier, I fell to the ground in a torrent of tears. At wit's end, feeling that there was nothing now that I could do, I cried out to the Lord. "Please, Lord, forgive me for not being a good friend! I was afraid and unsure. I didn't know what to do. I didn't help Marie, and now you've sent Faith. What can I do? I am so guilty! I don't want Faith to get hurt. It isn't her fault! She did nothing wrong. Please help me! Help me to be a better friend. I know now that I can't do this on my own." Wiping my eyes and slightly dazed, I saw myself get up and walk to the front door again. Just at that moment, Faith broke free from her tormentors and ran to open the door for me. She grabbed me by the shoulders and was shaking me.

"Wake up! Wake up!" Mom said as she put her arm around my shoulders, gently rocking me. "You're fine. It was only a nightmare."

I slowly opened my eyes and looked around the room. It was true. I was home in my own room. The light was just coming up in the sky.

What? I thought. *It wasn't real? But it felt so real, too real!* Then I realized that I would never know what Faith was about to tell me because it was just a dream.

I could tell that Mom wanted to talk, get some sort of explanation, but there was no time. I had just enough time to throw my clothes on and get to school for real. I got dressed, ran the brush through my hair, and was tossing my books into my bag when I saw the crumpled note again. Instinctively, I picked up my phone and took a couple of pictures of it. I could send the pictures to Dakota later so that she'd know what I was talking about.

Thankfully, I managed to make it to school before the first bell, sliding into my seat just as it rang.

Mrs. Hart took attendance, then asked us if we had thought about why the character was called Boo Radley and not just Boo. There had been so much going on that I had totally forgotten about English class and the novel.

I looked around the room, and no one else seemed ready with an answer either.

Mrs. Hart waited another minute and then began to call on people.

Oh no! I thought. *I hope somebody else has a good answer. Don't call on me. Don't call on me. Oh, please! Don't let her call on me!* I prayed silently.

Rachel was the first one Mrs. Hart asked, but she just shrugged her shoulders. Looking disappointed, Mrs. Hart then asked Aimee if she had thought about it. No, she hadn't. Next, she prompted Alyssa for an answer. Nothing there either.

Mrs. Hart had become irritated. "Young people, you need to take your education and homework assignments seriously. Since no one seems to have even given the question a second thought, from now on I will assign these types of questions as a graded essay assignment."

I could feel the frown on my face as I glanced at my classmates who were scowling. Out of the corner of my eye, I noticed Faith timidly raising her hand. After what felt like an eternity, Mrs. Hart noticed.

"Faith, why do you think the author included the character's last name?" Mrs. Hart asked.

"Umm, maybe to let us know that he is an adult and not a kid like Jem and Scout?" Faith answered with a question in her voice.

"That is a very good observation. Yes, Boo Radley is an adult, and including his last name does make that more clear," Mrs. Hart said.

"Any other ideas class?" asked Mrs. Hart as she scanned the room. "Okay, let me ask you a different question. Get a piece of paper and a pen. Make a list of what you think of, how you would describe, someone named Boo compared to someone named Boo Radley. You have three minutes, and then we'll discuss what you've written."

I quickly jotted down some of the things I remembered from the story, then passed it in to Mrs. Hart.

Boo	Boo Radley
monster, scary	has a family
unknown	had a job
never seen, invisible	lives in the house down the street
	people used to see him, knew what he looked like

To my surprise, she started to write the same chart on the board, saying, "Write this chart in your notebook. You will need it to write your homework essay tonight."

Soon, class was over, and I hurried to the restroom before the next hour began. Quickly, I entered the farthest stall and turned to close the door. That's when I saw it: disgusting words scrawled across the door to the stall and the wall in ugly, thick black marker, the permanent kind. Among the profanity, I could see *loser go home, sissy princess*, and *no one likes you*. I was so upset I wanted to cry. Who would do that? Why? Who were they aiming it at? I got out my phone and started taking pictures. Dakota would definitely know that I wasn't kidding about bullying when she saw those!

I finished up in the bathroom and was washing my hands when I heard Mrs. Strickland just outside the door in the hallway. She pushed open the door, saying, "Why is it that I need to come in here, Kate? Is someone not feeling well? Oh, Lacy! Are you okay?"

"I'm fine, Mrs. Strickland," I answered politely as I wiped my hands and went to leave.

I had just gotten into the corridor when I heard her bellow, "What is this world coming to!"

I quickly moved to the side as I heard her slam the door to the girls' restroom and watched her stride with purpose toward the principal's office, her pinched face as red as a fire engine. She glared at all of us as she strode past and instructed us in a commanding voice to go to class.

When I got to class, the gang was chattering in hushed voices. Faith was sitting at her desk by herself. Since Mrs. Strickland wasn't back from the principal's office yet, I went over to talk with her. I noticed that she was finishing last night's homework. It was strange that she didn't have the homework done. Faith always did all of her homework.

"Hi!" I said, trying to sound upbeat.

Faith kept writing hurriedly and mumbled, "Hi," barely looking in my direction.

I tried again, saying, "It's a good thing the test is next week instead of today, don't you think?"

"Uh huh."

You could hear a pin drop it was so silent in the room, which was unusual since the teacher wasn't there. I noticed that the other girls were acting strange, even for them. Though they were talking, you wouldn't know it because they were whispering so quietly. Every once in a while, I'd see one of them look over at us and point. I plunked myself in the desk next to Faith.

"I wonder what they are talking about over there," I whispered.

"Who cares!" retorted Faith. I could sense a feeling of angry resignation in her voice, which made me feel even more uncomfortable.

What is wrong with Faith? Why is she acting this way? I wondered.

A minute later, the gang raced back to their seats as we heard the *thump, thump, thump* of Mrs. Strickland's footsteps coming closer. She opened the door and let it close with a loud bang. It was as if all the air had been sucked out of the room as all of us collectively held our breath, not knowing what to expect next. Her eyes as cold as ice, Mrs. Strickland scanned the room silently. Her gaze stopped on Faith.

"Faith, go to the principal's office. Pastor Dave is waiting to speak with you," she said.

Surprised, Faith looked up from her work. "Me? The office? Why?" she stammered.

"Pastor Dave will discuss it with you," Mrs. Strickland answered coldly, not looking at Faith as she opened the door to usher her out of the room.

Faith got up from her seat and headed toward the door. Mrs. Strickland saw that she didn't have her books with her and added, "Bring all your belongings, as you won't be coming back to class."

Faith's face changed from a look of shock and confusion to utter dismay. Everyone was staring at her as she clumsily gathered her things as quickly as she could, dropping first her pen and then her books, tears starting to brim over her eyelids.

The door had barely closed when I heard the soft buzz of voices of the other girls behind me. "It was her! She did it!"

Mrs. Strickland spun around to face them. "Girls, stop whispering!" she said firmly.

Rachel raised her hand. "Why won't Faith be coming back?" she asked.

Then Aimee chimed in smugly before Mrs. Strickland could answer, "Faith vandalized the bathroom! That's why."

Mrs. Strickland put her hands up for silence. "Girls, it is not proper to discuss this," she said. "We are not to gossip. Now find your science fair partner and work together on your project."

Everyone moved to sit with their partner but me. My partner was in the office, likely bawling her eyes out. *Was that it?* I wondered. Were they blaming Faith for the writing in the girls' restroom? That was absurd. She would never do something like that, would she? Then I began to question myself. How did I know that she wouldn't do that? I mean, I really didn't know her that well, and she was upset with the girls in the class. Could that be her way of venting?

I tried to stop thinking about Faith and work on the project, but then I started hearing snippets of the other girls' conversations. "She's such a loser." "Hopefully, she'll just go back to Georgia." Aaargh! They really *were* mean!

It probably wasn't Faith who had written those awful things. Since I had no partner, I was supposed to be working on the project by myself, but it was next to impossible to concentrate. I looked over the research that Faith and I had already done. We basically had all the information we needed for the background research paper. The next step was to start the experiment. We already knew that we were going to ask the girls in the class to participate. I wished that Faith was with me to help, but she would understand. Besides, it would probably be super awkward right now for her to talk to them.

I approached Mrs. Strickland's desk to ask if I could start the experiment today and ask for the other girls' help. Since there was still a half an hour left in class, Mrs. Strickland said that I should definitely begin the interview phase of the project. I nodded and wondered who would be easiest to ask first. Who was the least witchy and would be willing to help?

I glanced over at Kate. She was usually okay, and she was smiling, so I made my way over to her desk. To my surprise, she thought that the project sounded cool and was happy to help. I asked her a few questions and had her write down some answers, noticing which hand that she used.

Wow! That was actually easy! I thought.

Next, I asked Aimee, who was helpful too.

I had interviewed almost half of them when I could see Rachel and Alyssa looking over at me. I was almost done asking Amanda the questions when they came over.

Rachel asked, "So, what's going on?"

Amanda happily answered, "Lacy is interviewing me for her science project about handedness. Cool, huh?"

Rachel and Alyssa exchanged a look that said, "We are the queen bees. Why didn't she ask us?"

Alyssa looked over at me. "How many people do you need for your experiment?"

"Oh! I just started today," I answered, looking up. "It would be great if you two could participate. There's just enough time before the bell rings."

They looked satisfied in their self-importance and sat down while Amanda finished writing the last answer.

"Uh, it looks like your pen is dead," said Amanda, shaking it and trying to scribble down the last word.

"That's the only pen I have." I frowned.

"No worries," Rachel said smugly as she pulled a black marker out of her purse.

I asked her my questions, noticing how gracefully the marker glided over the paper. Then she handed the pen to Alyssa.

"I don't know how you can write with these," Alyssa complained, pulling another chunkier marker out of her pencil case. "I can't get a grip on those fine-tip ones."

"Ali, you know that I always have the fine-tip ones to practice my calligraphy," Rachel replied.

"Yeah, yeah," Alyssa retorted, trying to ignore Rachel as she answered my questions.

I looked at the clock. "We can finish if we hurry," I said. "I only have one more question."

"Okay. No problem," Alyssa said.

The timing was perfect. Ali crossed the last *t* just as the bell rang.

The rest of the day was a blur. I moved from class to class in a fog, preoccupied with what was happening to Faith. I hadn't seen her since she left the room crying. How long was she in the principal's office? Did her mom come and speak with Pastor Dave too? Where was she now? Did she go home? I just wished I knew something! Why did she even get taken out of class? I saw Caleb in the hall a couple of times. The first time, I tried to wave to him, but he didn't see me. The second time, he looked away when I waved. What was going on?

The bell to dismiss school for the day rang. I hurried to Caleb's locker. I would find out! I would stand in front of his locker until he told me. I got there just before he did.

"Hi, Caleb!" I said.

"Hi," he answered gruffly. "I need to get into my locker."

"Caleb, I need to ask you something."

"Lacy, I don't have time for chitchat. Please move."

"No. Caleb, what happened to Faith?"

"Lacy, I said *move!*" he shouted and pushed me aside.

I landed on my bottom with a thud and watched in shock as Caleb rapidly shoved his books, notebooks, and binders into his knapsack and then slammed the door.

Feeling his anger and frustration, I began to cry softly. "Caleb," I whimpered.

He glared at me for a second and turned quickly to leave, his jaw set in a tight line and his neck and shoulders stiff, but then he turned around slowly and stopped to look at me.

"Oh, Lacy. I'm sorry. I didn't mean to make you cry. It's just ... just ..." Caleb put his book bag down and sat next to me.

I noticed then that his fists were clenched, his knuckles turning white. I wiped the tears off of my face with the back of my hand. "Faith had to leave early?" I ventured softly.

Caleb turned to me, his eyes blazing, grinding his teeth. "It's all their fault," he murmured through clenched teeth.

"All whose fault?" I asked.

Caleb just shook his head, and then his cell phone rang.

"Sure, Mom! I'm on my way now," he said as he picked up his things and headed toward the door.

Looking around, I realized that I was the only one left in the hallway. Everybody else had already cleared out. There wasn't a soul in sight. I slowly got up and went to the restroom. Mr. Jones was in there cleaning.

"Oh! Can I use the bathroom a minute?" I asked him.

"I suppose, but don't take too long. I have to finish cleaning before the program tonight. Can't leave that all over the wall for everybody to see, now can I?" he answered, clearly irritated that he had to do extra work.

It was the first time I had been back in there since Mrs. Strickland had found the profanity. Mr. Jones had already started to remove it from the stall. The black marker was now smeared so that the words were barely readable, and the cleaner he was using made the restroom smell awful.

"You almost done in there?" he called from the hallway.

"Yes!" I shouted nervously, then quickly blew my nose and washed my hands.

"Did ya see what they done in there? Who would do such a thing?"

I shrugged.

"I thought you was all good kids here," he continued sadly, shaking his head.

I just shrugged again and mumbled something about getting my books to go home.

"You go on then," he agreed. "Hurry! I need to lock the door before any other hooligans get in here to destroy the place."

I grabbed my books and headed outside to find Mom waiting

impatiently in the parking lot. "Lacy, why do you always have to be the last one to leave? You know that your grandma is waiting for us," she complained.

Oh, yeah! I'd forgotten that we were supposed to drive Grandma to her doctor's appointment that afternoon. Oh, well.

I decided to call Dakota when we got home. I couldn't talk to Mom. She was worried about Grandma and her upcoming medical tests. I was worried, too, about Grandma and Faith. There wasn't anything I could do to help Grandma right then, but maybe I could help Faith.

It looked to me like she was getting blamed for the vandalism in the girls' restroom, but there was no way that she did it, was there? I mean, why would she? She seemed fairly happy there. She had some friends, me and Kyle at least. She was doing well in school. Whenever test or quizzes were passed back, she always had an A, or at least a B+. As far as I could see, there was no reason for her to write all over the bathroom. Besides, she was super nice! I'd never heard her curse, and she rarely complained about anything. No. It definitely was not Faith who wrote those nasty things. But then, who was it? And how did no one see them doing it? I thought about that, going over it again and again in my mind while we sat in the waiting room at Grandma's doctor's office.

As soon as I got home to the privacy of my room I dialed Dakota's number, praying that she would pick up this time instead of her voice mail. One ring. Two rings. Three rings. I could feel my hope beginning to fade. I didn't want to leave another message. Where was Dakota anyway?

I was about to hang up when I heard, "Hello? Lacy, is that you?"

Hooray! Dakota picked up!

"Hi, sis! Yes, it's me," I answered.

"Good! I've been wanting to get back to you since I got your message. What's this about bullying? No one is picking on you, are they?" Dakota inquired in a concerned tone.

"No, not me," I answered quickly.

"Thank goodness!" she said with a sigh of relief.

There was a pause, and then she asked, "Lacy, you're not bullying anyone, right?"

I could tell from Dakota's serious tone of voice that she wasn't joking.

"Really? Really, Dakota? You think I would be the bully?" I asked, stunned.

"No, no … no, it's just … what else am I supposed to think? You said that you wanted to talk to me about bullying … so …"

"Dakota, it's the girls in my class who are the bullies. Remember they bullied Marie and Beth? Now I think they are bullying the new girl, Faith."

"Oh, and they never bullied you?" asked Dakota again.

"Well … no …" I started to reply.

"Um, Lacy, that doesn't sound too convincing. Have they been bullying you?"

"Not recently," I squeaked.

"Not recently!" exclaimed Dakota. "What do you mean? Did you tell anyone? Did you talk to Mom about this?"

"No. I didn't want anybody to know. It's embarrassing," I explained.

"Embarrassing? Why?" Dakota asked incredulously.

"Because … 'cause …" I stammered.

"Why are you protecting them?" Dakota demanded.

"Dakota, I'm not protecting anybody!" I blurted out angrily. "I just didn't want anyone to know that I don't have any friends!"

Oops! I hadn't meant to say that last part. Dakota wouldn't understand. She always had a bunch of friends. I wanted to cry then. I could feel the tears welling up in my eyes, my throat constricting.

"Lace … Lace?"

I wanted to answer her but was having a hard time battling back the tears.

"Lace, I'm sorry that I yelled at you," Dakota continued.

"Uh huh," I murmured so that she'd know I was still on the line.

"Lace, calm down. I know what you're going through," she said.

That was it! Miss Popularity was not going to preach at me!

"What? No way! You always have a bunch of friends. You are so friendly and so *not* awkward like me!" I exclaimed between sobs.

"Lace, Lace, listen to me. I *do* understand. Yeah, I always had a lot of people to hang out with and goof around with, but I never had a best friend to confide in. Remember, I always talked to you," she explained.

I stood silently for a moment, thinking. That was one of the reasons I missed Dakota so much. She always told me all about her day. She also told me her thoughts and dreams. It was fun, and she made me feel like a special part of her life.

"Lace, Lace? Did you hear me? Are you still there?" Dakota asked anxiously.

"Oh! Yeah, I'm still here," I answered.

"Do you see what I mean?" she continued. "I had fair-weather friends. They were there as long as everything was cool and we were having fun. I knew I couldn't rely on them if I had a problem."

"So, you don't think that I'm a loser too?" I asked quietly.

"What?" asked Dakota, astonished. "No way! Why would I ever think that?"

"Well, let me tell you everything that's been going on this year, and then you can tell me if I'm a loser or not," I said.

"Okay, Lace, but try to summarize. I mean, you must have homework, and I have a project to finish."

So I launched into my story about the gang and all the rotten things they had been doing. I even managed to give her a fairly concise synopsis of the Kyle situation. Everything was just such a tangled mess. I hoped that she could help me untangle at least some of it tonight. I finished my story by asking, "Okay, so now what should I do?"

"Whoa! You gotta give a girl time to process all that!" retorted Dakota. "Let me see if I have this all straight. I should have taken notes. First, you still like Kyle. Second, you made friends with the new girl, Faith. Third, the other girls make you feel left out. Am I right so far?"

"Yes, but the other girls do more than make me feel left out. I mean, that's bad, but it's worse than that."

"Worse than that? How?"

"Well, the drawings and notes they gave me made me feel ugly and stupid. I feel like they are always making fun of me."

"Did you keep any of those?"

"I don't know. Why would I want to keep them?" I asked defensively.

"Lace, I know that they are hurtful, but they are your evidence."

"Evidence?"

"Yes, evidence. With those, you can prove that they were bullying you. It's not just your word against theirs. Remember how we wished Marie had kept that picture of the bloody knife they gave her last year?"

"Uh huh."

I started sniffling. That was true. Marie had been so upset that she had thrown the picture away. When she finally told Mrs. Strickland about it, nobody believed her.

"Lace, you've got to look for those papers. Maybe you just threw them under the bed or in your locker or something. Promise me that you'll look for them," Dakota implored.

"Okay," I agreed, nodding, even though she couldn't see me.

"Lacy, do you know if Faith got any notes bullying her?"

I thought a minute. Yes! The note that Caleb had given me to look at was definitely a bullying note. I told Dakota about it.

"Do you still have it?" she asked with an urgency in her voice.

"I ... I don't know. I'm not sure if I gave it back to Caleb."

"Look for that one too," instructed Dakota.

"Dakota, I still don't know if, or how, I should help Faith," I whimpered.

"Help Faith?" she repeated questioningly.

"Yeah, I think that she was kicked out of school today," I stated before blowing my nose.

"Kicked out of school? But why?" Dakota asked, surprised.

"There was graffiti in the girls' restroom, and I think Faith is being blamed for writing it," I said sadly.

"What! Why didn't you tell me that?"

"I was going to. I just hadn't gotten to that part yet," I mumbled. "Besides, I didn't want to tell the story out of order."

"Lacy!"

"I know ..."

"Do you? That poor girl! You have to help her. I don't care if you think she took Kyle. She is in real trouble. You have to tell the teachers and the principal what you know."

"But, but, what if they don't believe me?"

"Lace, that's why you should find those notes. Look! Find them and then talk to me before you do anything, okay? Promise?"

"Okay, sis! I promise."

"Okay! You know that I'm always here for you, right?"

It was true. Dakota always had my back.

"Thanks, sis! I'll talk to you soon."

Everything was still a mess, but it was starting to look a little less tangled.

I got to school a few minutes early the next day. I wanted some time to talk with Caleb. I needed to know what was happening with Faith. When I walked in, I could see the gang huddled together by the freshmen lockers. They were whispering and laughing as usual. I looked past them down the hall. Caleb and Kyle were quietly discussing something, somber expressions on their faces. Faith was nowhere in sight.

I really need to talk to Caleb, I thought, *but Kyle is there.*

I hadn't spoken to Kyle since the fall festival. I felt so stupid, believing that he liked me and that he would be my boyfriend. I just didn't understand what had happened. Or maybe I did. Faith had happened, I thought, furrowing my brow and pursing my lips. There was no way that I could go over and talk to Caleb. It would be too awkward and weird with Kyle standing there. I decided to pretend to straighten my locker until the bell rang for class.

The school day started like any other, with Pastor Dave reading the scripture of the day over the intercom. "Thus Jesus instructed those assembled, 'So in everything, do to others what you would have them do to you, for this sums up the Law and the Prophets.' Matthew recorded Jesus's words that he spoke during his Sermon on the Mount. Please heed his words and put into practice this verse, Matthew 7:12. We should always treat others how we want to be treated, fairly and with respect, especially our brothers and sisters in Christ."

That was right! This was what Mom always said, "Do unto others as you would have them do unto you." I would want Faith to help me if I had been wrongly accused, wouldn't I? Thinking about it and feeling bad for her wasn't enough. I had to actually *do* something to right the wrong.

"Lacy, Lacy? Are you with us? We are discussing the novel now. Get out *To Kill a Mockingbird*." Mrs. Hart's voice jolted me out of my reverie.

I nodded mechanically and bent down to get my book from under my seat.

Mrs. Hart continued, "Class, I want you to work with your partner and brainstorm four questions about what you read last night."

I looked over at Rachel and smiled weakly. She was my partner this week. I picked up my book and notebook and moved to the seat next to her.

"So, we only need four questions," I said, trying to sound nonchalant. Secretly, I hoped she would already have some questions, because I only quickly looked over the reading the night before. Every time I'd try to focus on the story, I'd just wind up thinking about Faith, or Kyle, and how everything had gone wrong.

"What were we supposed to read?" Rachel asked.

Oh no! I thought. That was a question, but I knew that wasn't one of the questions Mrs. Hart would want. "We had to finish reading chapter 28," I answered coolly.

"Class, since chapters 27 and 28 work together, you can have questions concerning either or both chapters," Mrs. Hart's voice rang out over the hubbub.

"Mrs. Hart, do we have to know the answers to the questions?" asked Kate.

"No, you don't. We'll discuss the answers together," responded Mrs. Hart.

Oh, good! Then I'll write down these two, I thought and began writing, "What happens to Jem and Scout the night of the pageant?" and "Who carries Jem home?"

"There are my two questions. Here's the paper for you to write yours," I said as I pushed the paper toward Rachel.

She read my questions and then looked up questioningly. "Pageant? Like a beauty pageant?" she asked.

"No, a school pageant … sort of like a play for little kids," I explained.

"Oh! Did they wear costumes for the play?"

"Yeah, Scout did."

"Good!" she answered and quickly wrote, "What was Scout's pageant costume?" and "What was Scout's role in the pageant?"

Well, we had four questions at least. It seemed as soon as we had finished writing, Mrs. Hart was collecting the papers to look them over.

"We won't have time to go over all of the questions in class together. We'll concentrate on the questions dealing with the pageant, and you can answer the rest for homework," explained Mrs. Hart as she wrote the questions on the board.

Then she turned to ask us our thoughts. "Let's start with this question: 'What was Scout's pageant costume?'"

Blank stares followed the question.

"Does anyone here know what costume she wore?" Mrs. Hart prodded.

Silence.

"Okay, maybe the person who wrote the question will know the answer," said Mrs. Hart as she shuffled through the papers, looking for the author.

I glanced over at Rachel, who was filing her nails. Nope. She didn't know the answer.

"Let's see ... Rachel, you wrote the question. So, what was Scout's costume?" Mrs. Hart asked.

"Hmm ..." said Rachel thoughtfully. "A dog. Scout was a dog."

"No. Please remember that it was an agricultural pageant," responded Mrs. Hart.

"Aimee, do you know what Scout's costume was?"

Aimee shook her head and guessed, "A tomato?"

"No, not a tomato. Kate, do you know?"

"A pineapple!" Kate practically yelled.

"I appreciate your confidence, but that, too, is wrong."

"How about you, Amanda? Alyssa?" queried Mrs. Hart looking around the room.

"Mrs. Hart, is Scout's costume really that important?" asked Alyssa. "I mean, who cares if she was a dog or a pineapple?"

With a disheartened look on her face, Mrs. Hart answered firmly, "Yes, it does matter. Actually, how the costume was made matters more than what the costume was and what Scout's role in the pageant was."

Mrs. Hart scanned the room.

"Please raise your hand if you read last night's assignment," she requested.

Everybody raised their hand. Mrs. Hart looked surprised.

"Okay. Please, raise your hand if you read the *entire* assignment," she continued.

Only three students raised their hands.

"That's what I thought." Mrs. Hart sighed. "Get your book. We'll read the part about the pageant together and discuss it. You will have a quiz over this tomorrow."

I could feel myself scowling, thinking about having to read aloud in front of everyone and then having a quiz tomorrow too. I didn't have time to worry about English. I had to find those notes and help Faith.

"Lacy, please start reading the section for us," said Mrs. Hart, trying to smile and be positive even though I could tell that she was upset with all of us.

I began reading where Scout was preparing for the pageant, struggling to get into her costume. As I was reading, I heard a few snickers.

"Pork? She was pork?" said the girls, giggling.

"Yes, but notice how her costume is made," said Mrs. Hart. "Can she move easily in it? Can she see out of it?"

I kept reading, and we realized that it was a very uncomfortable costume made out of chicken wire. Scout couldn't move her arms from her sides, and she definitely couldn't see anything. It was decided that Jem would escort her to the school so that she didn't walk into anything. Their father, Atticus, was very tired after a long day in court—he was a lawyer—so he wasn't going to the pageant.

It was Rachel's turn to read next. I started to smile, as the funny parts were coming up in the story.

On the way to the school, Jem and Scout were surprised by their friend Cecil who jumped out from behind a tree to scare them. Then Scout missed her part in the pageant! She fell asleep backstage and then crashed onstage at the very end, making the audience burst into laughter. We were just about to get to the dramatic part of the chapter when the bell rang.

"Be sure to answer the rest of the questions for homework!" called Mrs. Hart as we filed out of the room.

I tried to look for Caleb as I made my way through the hall.

As I went to my locker to grab my books for the next class, I overhead some of the girls talking.

"Nope. She won't be back."

"Yeah, I talked to Mrs. Strickland about it."

"That's good. I didn't like her anyways."

"Good riddance!"

My stomach lurched. They were probably talking about Faith. What did Alyssa mean, she already talked to Mrs. Strickland about it? I wanted to go over and ask, but I knew she wouldn't tell me. She'd either ignore me or say that she was talking about something or somebody else.

Suddenly, I realized that the hallway was practically empty, and I was about to be late for class. No time to put my English stuff away; I'd just have to take it all to history with me. I slammed my locker shut and turned to book it to class. There was no way I wanted to do push-ups for being late. All I had to do was turn the corner, and the classroom was at the end of the hall. I could make it if I ran.

Obviously, I wasn't the only one running late. As I rounded the corner, I saw Kyle, or rather the blur of Kyle, as we looked at each other, panicked. Neither of us was able to stop before we collided with each other. Books and papers flew all over the floor, scattered in a mess around us as we sat there staring at each other, dazed.

"Kyle … I … I … didn't see… I mean…" I stammered.

"Lacy, I'm sorry," he said at the same time.

I could feel that my face had turned bright red. *He must think I'm an idiot klutz. That's why he likes Faith better than me.*

"Sorry, Lacy. Here, I'll help you pick up your stuff," he said.

We quickly gathered our things and hurried to class. Somehow, I still managed to get there on time, even if I was shaken and my things were all in a jumble. We were supposed to work on a project with our partner in class, but of course, my partner, Faith, was not there, so I had to work alone.

I went to get out my book and my notebook but couldn't find them. That had to be it there. I grabbed my blue notebook out of my bag. The notebook was blue, but where were my notes from yesterday? I began to flip through the pages. *That's not my handwriting.* Uh oh! I had Kyle's notebook! He must have mine then. We picked up the wrong ones in the hallway after our collision. I was about to set it down and just use one of my other notebooks when I thought I saw my name on one of the pages. The writing was like chicken scratch, but yes, it was definitely my name. Curious, I began to look at what was written on the other pages. There it was again. Just my name, over and over again. I flipped a few more pages. My name at the top of a note! Was he writing me a note? Should I read it? I mean, he didn't read my diary when he had the chance.

Just then, I saw Mrs. White walking over to see how the project was coming. I quickly turned the page so that she couldn't see the note. Mrs. White glanced over, saw the blank page, and said with a grimace, "Nothing yet? You'd better get a move on. Remember the project is due on Friday."

I nodded and said as politely as I could that Faith had our notebook and that she was absent.

Upon hearing that, Mrs. White snapped, "I suggest you get it from her then or start the project over yourself."

Rachel and Alyssa started giggling, so Mrs. White asked what was so funny.

"Nothing. Nothing at all," they replied amid stifled laughter.

Was Mrs. White trying to tell me that Faith was not coming back?

I picked up my history book to start the project again. What were all those papers doing stuffed into my book? *Don't tell me that I have Kyle's book too!* No, it was my history book, but Kyle had shoved his papers into my book in his haste: math homework, English notes, a biology quiz. *Hey! He got a 98 percent! I guess he's cute* and *smart*, I thought, smiling to myself. What was this? Another note, but this one was written by a girl, judging from the handwriting. I could feel my warm, happy feeling melt away, replaced with ones of suspicion and jealousy. I just had to know. Who had written him a note, and what did it say? I raised my hand to ask to use the restroom. I didn't want to read it in front of the gang. Besides, what if Mrs. White saw me reading a note? She might take it.

I hurried to the privacy of the bathroom to find out what was in the note.

Kyle,

Thanks for talking to me and being my friend. Since we moved here, I haven't made many friends, just you and Lacy. I don't know why. I thought it would be easier, but most of the girls in my class are kind of mean. I would confide in you more, but I don't want to gossip. Anyways, I just wanted to thank you for being there for me, for being a shoulder to cry on. I can always count on you to cheer me up and make me laugh even when I'm feeling down.

Faith

I read the note over again, letting the meaning of the words sink in. Faith only had me and Kyle for friends. She was lonely. I read the note a third time. She was sad because she didn't have many friends and because the other girls were mean. Kyle had only been trying to cheer her up those times I had seen them talking and laughing together. She wasn't trying to steal Kyle at all! Suddenly I felt awful for having suspected Faith. What a horrible friend I was! Faith needed me, and all I could do was worry about my own feelings. I shoved the note back into my pocket and quickly went back to class before I got in trouble for taking too long. I slipped into my seat and opened the notebook to work on the project, forgetting that it wasn't my notebook; it was Kyle's. Staring up at me from the page was a poem.

> The waves of your hair crash
> crimson and mahogany
> over your eyelash.
> Your eyes shine bright.
> I am dazzled by your light,
> Entranced by your smile,
> your song.
> Yours forever,
> Kyle

Next to the poem there was a picture of a girl with big bright eyes. Her brown hair cascaded gently over her shoulders. Highlighting the waves were barely visible flecks of red. A strand of her hair hung carelessly just over one eye. I just stared at the girl looking up at me from the page. She was pretty! Her eyes were friendly, and so was her slightly impish smile. I brushed the hair away from my eye with my hand and looked over my shoulder to make sure no one had seen as I quietly closed the notebook.

As soon as the bell rang, I booked it to the library to photocopy the poem, picture, and the note from Faith. I knew that Kyle would be looking for me to get his stuff back, so I couldn't wait to copy these later. I *needed* to have them for myself to keep forever! I got to the photocopier just as Tim was finishing copying some notes.

"Oh, hi, Lacy."

"Hi, Tim. You done?"

"Oh, yeah. Go ahead."

I put the money in and reached for the notebook.

"What cha copying?" asked Tim.

I tried to stay cool. I didn't want him to know that it was Kyle's notebook. "Just some notes."

"Oh. Yeah, I just copied notes that I missed from Matt. Hey, what's that on the floor?" he asked as he bent over to pick it up. "It looks like a note."

Alarm bells went off in my head. *The note from Faith to Kyle! I can't let anyone know that I saw it!*

"Oh, that must have fallen out of the notebook. Thanks," I said as nonchalantly as possible as I snatched it out of his hand.

"No problem. Well, talk to you later," called Tim as he strode out of the library.

Whew! That was a close one! I thought as I unfolded the note and placed it on the photocopier. Before I could turn back to the copier to retrieve the note, I heard another familiar, though hurried voice.

"Lacy, there you are! I've been looking all over for you!"

"Looking for me?" I asked as I swiped the note off of the copier and crammed it into my pocket.

"Yeah, I think you have my notebook. I took out my notebook for English, but my notes weren't in there, just history stuff."

"Oh, yeah. I guess we must have switched notebooks by accident. Sorry, I didn't notice," I said sheepishly, looking through my bag. I didn't want him to know that I saw the poem or the drawing. It wasn't a lie, was it? I mean, I hadn't noticed in the hallway. "Kyle, what does it look like?"

"There, it's that blue one. Thanks."

And just like that, he was gone. I stood there in a daze as the bell rang for lunch. At least I wouldn't be late to class. I gathered my things and walked slowly toward the hallway. The door to the library swung open just as I reached it. Caleb burst in, knocking me to the ground. Without stopping, he turned angrily and shouted, "Watch where you're going!" I couldn't believe he had just done that. I sat there stunned, literally seeing stars and hearing little birdies chirp as I tried to regain my composure.

The librarian hurried over to help me up. "Lacy! Oh dear, are you all right?"

"I ... I ... don't know," I stammered as I tried to figure out what exactly had happened. A crowd was beginning to gather around me.

"Everyone, back up! Give her some room!" instructed Ms. Martin. "Can you stand up? Do you feel dizzy?" asked the librarian.

Everything was a bit blurry, but I could hear the other students talking around me.

"Did you see that?"

"Yeah, Caleb just opened the door and slammed into her. Didn't even help her up."

"Do you blame him after what she did to his sister?"

"Yeah, it's all her fault that she's getting kicked out of school."

Wait! What! I tried to quickly turn my head to see who had said that, but moving so quickly made my head spin, and I had to lie down. I was getting blamed for Faith being expelled? How? Who was blaming me? What did I do?

The gossip continued: "Whoa, really? I thought Lacy and Faith were friends."

"Well, I guess not 'cause she ratted Faith out. She told the teachers that it was Faith who wrote all over the bathroom."

I wanted to yell, to scream, "No! No, you have it all wrong! I never said that Faith did it. It wasn't Faith! Faith is my friend."

Ms. Martin interrupted my thoughts. "Do you need to go the nurse?" she asked gently.

I nodded yes, and she began helping me up. "Come on. I'll go with you," she said kindly, then told everyone else to go back to class. I was still wondering how anyone would ever believe that I would implicate Faith as the vandal. Then I overheard the sophomore girls :"Sue, that can't be true. Lacy wouldn't do that."

"No, no, it is. I heard Rachel and Alyssa talking. When I asked them, they said that's what happened."

I leaned on Ms. Martin for support as we walked toward the nurse's office. She kept asking me questions, trying to make sure I didn't have a concussion. Ms. Martin was being very kind, but I couldn't stop thinking about what an awful mess the situation was. My head was reeling, more from what I'd heard than the fall. Why would anyone believe that I would say that about Faith? I was seething inside at the thought of Rachel and Alyssa lying about Faith—and now me too! *And Caleb thinks that I set up his sister.* I definitely couldn't count on getting any help from him to straighten things out. I would have to do it all by myself.

When I got home, I was determined to find all the notes and gather all the evidence. I emptied my backpack on my bedroom floor. I looked through all of my folders, binders, books, and notebooks, but not one of the notes was there. Maybe I had stuck them in one of my desk drawers? A half an hour later, I found my old diary, some birthday cards from Jade and my grandma, and some pictures from last year. *Well, where could they be? I know that I didn't throw them out, did I?* I decided to look in the box where I put my keepsakes, things I wanted to remember. I really doubted that any of them would be there (why would I *want* to remember that horrible stuff?), but I thought I'd look anyway. I opened the box: notes Jade had written me, the picture of Kyle and me at the fall festival (wow, that felt like it was forever ago now!), ticket stubs from movies and concerts that I had gone to. Nope, no mean notes and pictures in there either. *What am I going to do? I need those notes as evidence to prove that Faith is innocent.*

I got my phone to call Dakota for some advice. I could send her the pictures of the writing on the bathroom walls and see what she thought. The pictures! *That's right, I still have the pictures of the vandalism. They would be evidence, wouldn't they?* I looked at the pictures again. The handwriting definitely didn't look like Faith's. Had the principal even checked, or was he simply taking everyone's word as truth that Faith had done it? If it wasn't Faith's writing, then whose was it? It looked kind of familiar, but I couldn't say for sure. It was definitely a girl's handwriting though; the style was really round and loopy.

I wracked my brain for a good half an hour trying to figure out where I had seen the handwriting before, when I noticed the time; it was almost 8:00 p.m. *Oh no! I had better get some work done on the science project for tomorrow. I'm already behind since I have to do the whole project by myself now.* I would have to go back to the library to get some of the background information again, but thankfully I still had a few notes and the questionnaire samples that the girls in our class had finished. Now I only needed to ask a few more people to have an adequate sample set. I began shuffling through the questionnaires and taking notes.

I was about to pick up Rachel's questionnaire when I heard the phone ring. I waited a minute to see if it was for me. I could hear Mom's muffled voice from downstairs. I thought I heard my name, but then I didn't hear it again. A few minutes later, Mom knocked on the door to my room. When I opened it, she looked at me, a worried expression on her face. She said that she knew I was working on homework, but she needed to speak with me. It was Faith's mom on the phone. She was very upset over what had happened at school and apologized for Caleb's behavior. Mom sat on the edge of the bed and asked me if everything was okay. I didn't know how to answer. Should I tell Mom everything? Usually I confided in Dakota, but she wasn't there. I sat down uncomfortably at my desk chair. I didn't want to upset my mom, but if I didn't tell her some of what had happened, she would have been mad.

"Lacy, I hope you know that you can tell me anything," Mom said gently. "Faith's mom called to see if you are all right. She said that Caleb bumped into you accidentally," continued Mom with a question in her voice.

"I … I'm fine," I answered slowly.

"So it's true then? Caleb did bump into you?"

"Yes, I fell, but the librarian helped me up. I'm okay."

"Lacy, Mrs. Barrett said Caleb and Faith are both very upset by what has been going on at school. Do you know what would bother them?" asked Mom.

The whole time, I had been thinking how unfair it was that Faith was being blamed for the vandalism. I scooped my phone up off of my desk and thrust it toward Mom. "This, this is what they are so upset about!" I practically yelled.

"What are you trying to show me?" asked Mom, looking confused.

"Just look at the pictures," I said emphatically.

"Well, what is it?"

"Those are pictures of the graffiti in the girls' bathroom at school," I said soberly.

"Graffiti in the girls' bathroom?" Mom repeated, still not understanding.

"Yes. Faith is being blamed for it! They kicked her out of school!" I cried.

"Oh! Well, did she do it?" asked Mom.

"No! I mean … I really doubt it. Why would she?"

"Maybe she is unhappy here."

"Mom, I still don't think she would do a thing like that! She is way too nice."

"Lacy, I know that you two were friends, but honestly, you don't know her that well," said Mom, trying to be logical.

"Mom, she wouldn't do that," I said through clenched teeth.

"How do you know?"

"I told you. She is nice. She defended me in English class once," I blurted out.

"Wait! She defended you? What do you mean?" asked Mom, suddenly more agitated.

Crap. I hadn't meant to say that. I really didn't want to have to explain everything. *Mom wouldn't understand. She thinks that the gang are sweet, Christian young ladies.*

"Oh, it was nothing," I murmured.

"Obviously it wasn't to you, since you remember it and bothered to mention it," responded Mom.

There was no getting out of it; I could tell that Mom wasn't going to let it go without a discussion.

"Faith basically just told the other girls in the class that they were wrong for being mean to me."

"Being mean to you? Who was mean to you?" I could tell by the look on Mom's face that she was upset. "Lacy, why didn't you ever tell us that there was a problem?" asked Mom with a hurt look on her face.

"I ... I ... don't know. I mean ... it wasn't a big deal." I knew I was lying, or was I? *Everyone gets picked on, right?*

"Lacy, tell me now. What happened?" said Mom sternly. "How can we help you if you don't tell us anything?" queried Mom as she gently put her hand on my shoulder. I turned again to face her and burst into tears, thinking about how awful the gang had been to Marie, Marie Beth, me, and now especially to Faith. Mom gave me a hug. "It's okay, Lacy. You can tell me," she said as she handed me some tissues. For the next hour, I spilled my guts. I told her everything from last year and this year. Mom sat on the edge of my bed in shock, a few tears rolling down her cheek.

"Oh, honey! I'm so sorry! I had no idea," said Mom regretfully.

"So I lost my two best friends, and now the gang has had my new friend expelled. They even made it look like I was the one that ratted her out! That's why Caleb didn't care that he knocked me down," I cried.

"Lacy, I'm confused. What do you mean you ratted her out? You told me that she wouldn't do something like that."

"I know! But Rachel and Alyssa told everyone that I reported her as the vandal!" I wailed.

"But you didn't."

"I know that, but that's not what everyone else thinks. They think they know that I told on her. I need to do something to prove that Faith is innocent."

Mom sat silently for a few moments. I couldn't tell what she was thinking. An awkward silence hung in the air as I wiped my tears and reached for another tissue to blow my nose. Usually she would tell me to stay out of other people's business, or that it didn't involve me, so I shouldn't stick my nose where it didn't belong. This time though, as she turned to leave, she hugged me, saying, "Lacy, you are growing up. You know right from wrong. I will leave the decision to help Faith up to you as long as you realize that there will be consequences whether you help her or not. Remember that you should always be faithful to the truth. Right now, it is getting late. We can talk more about this tomorrow."

I nodded and started to get ready for bed. I washed my face and brushed my teeth, but I didn't stop thinking about my dilemma. Mom was right; there would be consequences if I helped Faith or if I chose to do nothing, like I found out last year. If I said nothing, Faith would be gone, and I would lose another friend. Also, my reputation would be ruined since everyone thought I told on her. *Everyone thinks I am a horrible friend.* I almost started to cry again when I thought about it. "I am not horrible!" my brain screamed. *I will help her. If—I mean when—I do, everyone will know that I'm a good friend who has your back.* Faith and I would be friends again (I hoped), and she would stay at the school. Of course, the gang wouldn't like me for helping Faith and outing them as liars, but it was clear already they didn't like me, so what did I have to lose? Now I just had to figure out a way to prove to the school that my words were the truth.

I was finally about to doze off when my phone buzzed. *Who could it be at this time of night?* I wondered. I rolled over to look at my phone sitting on the nightstand. Ugh! It was just an update for the game I liked to play online. *I should just turn the phone off,* I thought, but then the text message icon caught my eye. Someone had sent me a message, and I hadn't heard the phone go off. It was Faith. She must have texted me when I was talking with Mom. "Hi. Sorry that you have to do the science project by yourself."

What should I do? I mean, would she still be awake? This is so awkward. What should I say? Does Faith think that I accused her of the vandalism? Is she mad at me? Why did she even text me? Afraid to answer her, but more afraid not to, I typed, "Yeah, aren't u coming back 2 school?"

Five minutes passed, then ten. A half an hour later, I decided that Faith wasn't going to reply, at least not that night—and then my phone buzzed again. I hurriedly looked to find the message, but there was no message from Faith. Instead, Jade was texting me: "Hey girl! Just finished my history paper. Woohoo!" I smiled. That was so Jade. I quickly replied with a smiley face and a thumbs-up. I would have to get her input on the whole Faith situation the next day. I put my phone down and pulled the covers up to my chin.

Buzz-buzz, buzz-buzz. My phone was going off again. I rolled over to see who it was. This time, it was Faith. "Caleb says that you were the one who said I wrote all over the girls' bathroom."

I grabbed the phone and began typing furiously: "No, no, I didn't. Someone started a rumor." I held my breath, hoping that Faith would reply, that she would understand.

Buzz-buzz. "He says that everyone is saying that you told Mrs. Strickland that I did it."

I typed as fast as I could. "No, I never talked to Mrs. Strickland about it. Who told him that?"

A few seconds passed, then a couple of minutes. No answer. Why wasn't she answering me? I got out of bed and started pacing up and down my room. Every once in a while, I would look at my phone to make sure it was still on. Didn't she believe me? Why didn't she just tell me who said it? My phone screen lit up as it buzzed again: "I can't tell you."

What did she mean, she couldn't tell me? *It's about me! I have a right to know!* I wanted to yell at her, but we were texting. Besides, what good would yelling at her do? Hastily, I picked up my phone. "Why not?" I asked.

Miraculously, she replied right away. "Caleb made me promise not to." What! I could feel the anger rise up inside me. Who was Caleb protecting and why? This person was obviously a liar. I decided to try asking again.

"Faith, I need to know so I can get this all straightened out. Please tell me."

I paced some more, praying that she would name the culprit, but instead she said, "It's midnight. Mom is making me go to bed. Bye."

That was it? Just *bye*? I had to go to bed too, but how in the world could I sleep? Caleb was protecting the person who started the rumor about me. How would I find out who it was and prove that both Faith and I were innocent victims?

Bam! Bam! Bam! After tossing and turning most of the night, I was not happy to hear my alarm going off. Ugh! I groaned. I wanted to cry. Did I really have to get up and go to school to face the continuing drama? Yes! Yes, I did, and I would! I willed myself out of bed, determined to resolve the problem. I had to force myself to think positively. Everyone was always talking about the power of positive thinking. That's what I would do, be positive and pray. I suddenly had the urge to pray about the situation. I got down on my knees besides my bed and began to pray. "Lord, I know that I don't pray as often as I should, so I'm not sure that I'm even doing this right. I'm thankful for who you are and what you have done for us through Jesus Christ your Son. You are holy and righteous. I ask in Jesus's name that the problems at school with the gang be solved. You are all-knowing. You know who are blameless in this. You are a God of justice. Please help the innocent and serve justice upon the wrongdoers, that they may realize and learn from their error. Thank you." As I finished my prayer, I felt a wave of peace wash over me. Even though I was tired from not sleeping the night before, incredibly, I felt refreshed and ready to face the day.

We pulled up to the school just as Caleb was walking in. Kyle was waiting for him at the main door, and they walked in together talking. Part of me wanted to catch up to them, but another small voice inside me was saying that I'd better not, not yet anyway. The day progressed as usual; nothing was out of the ordinary. I tried to focus on classwork, but I kept waiting for something to happen, for some clue that would provide the answer to the problem and prove Faith's innocence. Then it happened. The fire alarm went off in the middle of lunch; one of the middle schoolers had forgotten to add water to their macaroni and cheese before putting it in the microwave. Smoke poured from the machine and begin to fill the cafeteria as we hurried outside into the parking lot. Everybody found their friends and hung out, enjoying the fresh air outside until the firemen gave the all clear. I overheard Caleb thanking Kyle for letting him know as I walked past them toward the old oak tree. *Letting him know what?* I wondered. I desperately wanted to ask them but somehow knew that neither of them would give me a straight answer at that point. I continued over to the tree where Mr. Grimes was talking with Mrs. Strickland.

"Shame about that girl Faith," Mr. Grimes said in his usual gruff manner.

Mrs. Strickland immediately stood up taller, throwing her shoulders back. "Why do you say that?" she asked, trying to sound casual.

"It's just a shame. She seems like such a nice girl," replied Mr. Grimes.

"Oh, appearances can be deceiving," retorted Mrs. Strickland.

"Well, I'm just surprised is all. I never had any trouble with her in my class, not even a late homework. Let's just say that I wouldn't have guessed that she would vandalize school property. She isn't the type," answered Mr. Grimes with a sidelong glance.

Mrs. Strickland was checking names off on her roster sheet, ignoring his last comment.

"Say, how did you come to the conclusion that she was the one who did it? Did she admit to it?" asked Mr. Grimes pointedly.

Mrs. Strickland's head jerked up at that. "It was obvious from what was written," she answered flatly.

Mr. Grimes repeated his question. "So, she admitted to having written the graffiti?" he persisted.

Mrs. Strickland fidgeted from one foot to the other and thumbed through her grade book uncomfortably. She could feel his penetrating gaze even though her eyes were scanning the book in her hands.

"Well, if she admitted it, I suppose there's nothing we can do but expel her," continued Mr. Grimes, a hint of sadness in his voice.

Mrs. Strickland looked up and blurted out defensively, "No, she did not admit to having committed the vandalism. However, I have it on very good authority from more than one witness that it was her."

"Oh," responded Mr. Grimes, taken off guard. "Well, then it sounds like someone is lying then if she said she didn't do it and someone else says that she did."

Exasperated, Mrs. Strickland retorted indignantly, "I highly doubt that my sources are lying. I have known those students for years."

The last I heard of their conversation was Mr. Grimes asking "Who?" before the fire engines roared up to the school with their horns blaring. I strained to hear Mrs. Strickland's answer, to no avail. How I wished I could read lips! It looked like she said three names, one, two and three syllables each. If only that fire truck wasn't so loud! I was so close to knowing who framed Faith!

I texted Dakota as soon as I got home. She would know what to do.

Instead of texting back, she called, and before I could even start filling her in on what happened, she hit me with a barrage of questions: "Did you find those notes and letters? Have you shown them to the principal yet? How's Faith doing? Have you talked to her? You should tell Mom. You have told Mom, right?" So many questions all at once! I was afraid to tell her that I hadn't found the notes, but I knew I had to. I held the phone away from my ear as she yelled, "What? You need those! I know you; you don't throw anything away. Find those right now. Do you hear me?! Lacy, answer me! Lacy!"

I picked the phone back up. "Yeah, Dakota, I know."

"You know? Then why haven't you found them yet?" Dakota demanded.

Now I was beginning to get angry. Did she think I was an idiot? Of course I knew that the notes were important, but everything was happening at once, and I still had to go to school and do my homework. "Dakota, Dakota …" My voice trailed off.

"What?" she asked, sounding irritated.

"I'm not stupid," I mumbled.

"Lacy, speak up. I can't hear you."

"I said I'm not stupid!" I yelled into the phone.

"Um, nobody said you're stupid," Dakota snapped back.

"Well, stop treating me like I am!"

"Huh? Look, I know that this is hard on you. Just find those papers, then call me back. Okay?" responded Dakota in a milder voice.

"Okay," I agreed, holding back tears as I hung up the phone. *Who does she think she is anyway to be able to yell at me like that? I know I have to find those notes.* I began to search my room. I looked in my backpack, in my desk, and on the bookshelf. I found nothing, not one note. Dakota was right though. I never threw anything away. I held on to everything for sentimental reasons, or to make a craft with, or maybe because, to be honest, I was just really bad at cleaning my room. Frantically I tore through one bin and then another. I emptied the bookshelves in case the papers were under or behind the books. I flipped through each book to see if maybe the papers had gotten tucked in between the pages. I dumped out three, no four, tote bags filled with old toys, game pieces, and doll clothes. I had to find those notes! I would not stop until I had them in my hand! The closet, I hadn't looked in the closet yet. I checked the pockets of all my sweaters, but all that was there was some gum, a few bobby pins, and a used tissue—gross. I looked in my sewing bag full of scrap material and ribbons, hoping for a miracle. There was blue, red-checkered, flowered, and pink fabric and five types of ribbon—but no notes. Toward the back of my closet, I noticed some of my pocketbooks. *Aha!* I thought. *I must have left them, or at least one of them, in my pocketbook.* I pulled them out and rifled through them, still coming up empty. From my vantage point in the middle of the room, it looked like a bomb had exploded. Books, clothes, toys, games, puzzle pieces, everything was strewn about everywhere. I felt stupid and desperate. Why hadn't I just been more careful with them! I was so glad Dakota wasn't there to see it. I really wanted to cry again. Nothing was working out. I felt so helpless.

Then I heard a soft knock at my door. *Oh no!* I thought. *Mom is going to see this and go through the roof!* I wanted to pretend that I wasn't there, hide, something, but if I moved one muscle, an avalanche of stuff would come crashing down. I crossed my fingers. Maybe she would just go away. I heard the knock again. A little louder this time.

Resignedly, I called out, "Come in if you dare!" The knob turned, and the door moved ever so slightly. "I said come in!" I shouted.

There was a muffled voice from the other side of the door. "I'm trying!" Indeed, she was trying. I could see that she was pushing on the door, but it wasn't going anywhere.

"Hold on!" I yelled as I stood up and plowed my way over through all of my stuff. "Wait a minute! There's something blocking the door," I said as I began grabbing handfuls of my random disorder and tossing it out of the way. "Okay, you should be good now."

Cautiously, the door was pushed open, and to my horror and joy, Jade was standing there with my mom. Both of them stood there with their mouths agape, looking at what was supposed to be my room. "I … I … I …" I started, even though I had no idea what I was going to say. I was so embarrassed.

My mom recovered from the shock first, spinning on her heel and shaking her head while she mumbled, "Not a word. No, I'm not going to say a word," as she started down the stairs. I looked over at Jade, and suddenly all of my pent-up emotions and stress came tumbling out as I began laughing hysterically. The next thing I knew, we were both laughing so hard there were tears streaming down our faces.

"What happened, Lacy?" asked Jade between fits of laughter. "It looks like a tornado hit."

"Yeah," I said, laughing, "or maybe a nuclear explosion." Then we laughed even harder. "Wait, before you come in, you'll have to sign a disclaimer waiving your right to sue me if you are hurt."

"Stop … stop … Lacy, I'm laughing so hard my stomach hurts!"

I paused a moment to look around. "Hmmm … I know I saw that form a minute ago." I turned to look at Jade, and we both burst out laughing again.

Although Jade was shocked to see my room a mess, it wasn't like she had never seen it messy, just never this bad. "So, I can come in?" she asked.

"Sure, but it's at your own risk," I joked.

"Why? There's no bugs or dirty underwear in here is there?"

"Hey, I haven't had dirty underwear in my room for at least six months." I laughed, remembering when we were in first grade and Jade had found my dirty undies thrown in with the doll clothes. I had been mortified and begged Mom for a hamper after that.

"So, what cha looking for?" asked Jade, looking me straight in the eyes.

"And this is why we're best friends. Only you would know that from looking at this pigsty."

"Mm-hmmm. Now tell me what you're looking for."

With a heavy heart, I told Jade how I needed to find the drawings and notes the gang had given to us. It was the proof of their bullying. Jade nodded, totally understanding how important it was.

"Lacy, I'll help you look. I knew that Faith wasn't in school anymore, but I didn't know why."

"Hey, how did you know?"

"My mom was talking with your mom at the supermarket. She asked how school was going, and your mom said that you were upset that the new girl isn't there anymore."

"Oh," I said quietly, looking at where the floor should be underneath the piles of junk.

"That's when I decided I would come over and cheer you up!"

"Aww, you're such a great friend!" I said as I hugged her.

Jade scanned the room and asked, "So, where do we start?" Then we looked at each other again and laughed. Two hours later, we had everything picked up and put back where it belonged, but we still hadn't found the notes. I felt defeated. I had just spent over three hours of my life searching for those stupid notes. I was so mad at myself for losing them, or throwing them away, or whatever I'd done with them.

Grr. Grr.

"Jade, what's that noise? Did you hear it?"

Jade started to turn slightly pink. "Uh, that's my stomach." *Grr. Grr.* "Yup, definitely my stomach," she said with a slight grin.

"Are you hungry? Oh no! Is it really that late? We missed dinner!" I rambled and realized that my stomach hurt too. "Let's go down and see what's in the fridge."

"Okay, I'll just let my mom know that I'm eating over here," said Jade as she texted.

"Hey, why don't you ask if you can stay over? My mom can bring you to school in the morning."

"Cool. Okay."

It would be like old times, a sleepover with Jade! I would just ask Mom for linens for the trundle under my bed, and voilà! We'd be all set.

Within half an hour, we ate, and Jade's mom came by with her stuff. She seemed happy to see me and gave me a big hug. It *was* just like old times! As soon as she left, Jade and I grabbed some cupcakes and smuggled them up to my room. Sticky followed us, jumping up and yapping. "Shh!" I scolded. "Be quiet!" I picked Sticky up, and we raced to my room before Mom could see that we had food with us. Jade dropped her things by my desk, and I went over to pull the trundle bed out. I pulled and pulled, but it wouldn't budge. Jade came over to help. Both of us were tugging and pulling on the handles, but nothing was happening.

"Ha-ha, I guess it's stuck because it hasn't been used in a while," I said sheepishly. "Let's try one more time before I have to go get Mom."

Five minutes later, out of breath and laughing, we fell back onto the floor, each of us with one of the handles in our hands. Oops. It was funny now, but what would my parents say?

"Why does Sticky have a cupcake wrapper?" I suddenly heard Mom ask.

"Huh?" Somehow I didn't think that would be her reaction. I looked up at the doorway to see her standing there holding a half-chewed wrapper. Then it hit me, the cupcakes! Sticky had jumped up and gotten them off of the desk when we weren't paying attention. I turned to look. Sure enough, the plate wasn't there. It was on the floor, and two of the cupcakes were missing.

"I'm sorry, Mom. At least the cupcakes weren't chocolate. We were trying to pull out the trundle bed for Jade. It's stuck," I explained.

That's when Mom looked and noticed that we were both holding a handle that used to be attached to the bed. I waited for her to yell at me, punish me for having broken the furniture. Instead, she grimaced and walked out of the room, calling Dad to come upstairs. I turned to Jade, a scared expression on my face. It was always worse if Mom asked Dad to hand down the punishment. That meant that she was too angry to deal with it. Neither one of us said a word. We could hear my dad tromp up the stairs with Sticky barking right behind him.

Dad came in shaking his head. "It looks like you girls don't know your own strength," he commented with a half smile on his face. Whew! At least Dad wasn't really angry. I told him what had happened and began to relax a little, unclenching my fists.

"Well, let me have a look at it," he said and began trying to pry open the trundle with his fingers. "No, that is definitely jammed tight. I'll have to go get some tools." He came back a few minutes later with his toolbox. "Now, since you two are so strong, you can help me tip the bed over so I can see what the matter might be from the underside. Okay, on the count of three. One, two, three!"

With the three of us lifting it, the bed seemed light. It was no problem at all. Dad got his flashlight and started checking the slide mechanism of the bed. He said it was like a drawer, and maybe one of the hinges that held it to the rest of the bed was busted. Nope, those seemed to be fine. He ran his fingers along the space where the bed and the trundle met. "Aha!" he cried in triumph. "This is your culprit." He pulled out a plastic bag that had gotten caught between the metal runner and the hinge. "Let's turn it back over and see if it opens now." We helped turn it over, and he tested the trundle. "Ta-da! It glides like it's brand-new. Too bad about the handles. I'll have to put them back on later."

"Thanks, Dad! Do you want a cupcake?" I asked, offering him the plate.

"No, no. From what I've heard, Sticky has already taste tested those. I'll find another snack in the kitchen." Dad chuckled as he headed downstairs.

"I'll go get the linens," I told Jade and went to the hall closet. I came back and picked up the bag that had been stuck in the bed. "I know that you don't want that dusty thing on there," I said and whisked it away. I began to crumple it up to throw it away when I noticed that there was something in the bag. I stuck my hand in and pulled out some papers. There were the notes and drawings for which I had been searching!

"Jade, Jade, look!" I cried. She hurried over to see what I was holding. "Super! You found them!"

"Weird, huh? I don't know how they wound up stuck there, but at least I have them now."

Jade was looking at them intently: the drawing of me with a face full of acne getting pelted with volleyballs and the note Faith got in her locker. I thought a minute. Had I told Jade about the graffiti in the girls' bathroom? I grabbed my phone and showed her the pictures.

"This is why Faith isn't at school anymore," I said, holding back tears. Jade looked up at me wide-eyed.

I continued, "I'm 99 percent sure that she didn't do it, and the worst part is that she thinks I ratted her out."

Jade's jaw just about hit the floor then "You? She thinks you'd do that? Why would she think that?" asked Jade incredulously.

"Somebody, or somebodies, told her brother that I did. Now they are both mad at me," I said wringing my hands. "Jade, that's why I wanted to find the notes so badly, so I can use them as evidence that we were both being bullied."

"Yeah, duh, I know. So they were bullying both of you. So what? How does that prove that Faith didn't write that stuff in the bathroom?"

I had been concentrating so much on finding the notes I hadn't thought about how exactly having them would help. "I ... I don't know," I stammered in bewilderment. "Dakota just told me to find them, that they were the proof."

"Do you have any more?"

"No ... well, it really isn't a mean note. I found a note that Faith wrote to Kyle ..."

Jade jumped off of the bed before I could finish. "What! Why didn't you tell me? What does it say?"

I went over to my backpack and got it out. "Look, I have a copy of it."

Jade grabbed it out of my hands and quickly read it. "That poor girl! You and Kyle are her only friends, and you thought she was trying to steal him from you!"

"I know, I know," I answered guiltily. "I feel horrible for thinking that." I paused a moment. "So, do you think the notes are proof?"

"I guess. They do show that you were being bullied. Faith even says in her note that the other girls are mean."

"But it still doesn't prove that it wasn't Faith who vandalized the restroom, does it?" I asked, disheartened.

Jade started nodding her head then stopped. "Wait a minute. Let me see those pictures again."

I handed her my phone. "Look, look at the writing in the pictures and compare it to Faith's writing in the note. Do they look similar to you?"

"No … but… Oh! You're right! They don't look the same at all!" I said, a smile spreading across my face. "This will prove that Faith didn't do it, right?"

"I think so, but will the principal listen?"

"He has to! The evidence is right there. Oh, but what about the other 'witnesses'?"

It seemed like I had just closed my eyes when the alarm went off. Jade and I had stayed up trying to figure out who the witnesses were, so maybe I really had just closed my eyes. I didn't know if I'd slept a few hours or at all. Mom dropped Jade off at her school and then brought me to school. Caleb and Kyle were hanging out in the hallway talking. I waved, but they ignored me. *Caleb must still be mad at me*, I thought. *Well, he won't be helpful in figuring out this mess.* I made my way to English class. We were still working on *To Kill a Mockingbird*.

"Do you all remember when we discussed the meaning of the title of the novel?" Mrs. Hart asked.

A few of us nodded rather warily. I hoped there wouldn't be a pop quiz.

"So, tell me then, according to the story, is it good to kill a mockingbird?" continued Mrs. Hart.

Amanda's hand shot up. "It's wrong to kill anything. It's against the Ten Commandments."

"Yes," Mrs. Hart conceded, "but what reason is given according to the novel not to kill a mockingbird specifically?"

She waited a minute or so for us to answer. I looked around the room and noticed the rhythmic ticktock of the clock. "You can look back in your notes," Mrs. Hart reminded us. "It's not a quiz." Backpacks unzipped, and papers rustled as everyone got out their notebooks to at least pretend to look for the answer. I flipped through my notebook, hoping that I had written down what Mrs. Hart wanted since it sounded important.

I was about to raise my hand when I heard Aimee blurt out, "Jem's dad told him it was a sin to kill a mockingbird."

"That's right," agreed Mrs. Hart. "He did say that. Why did he say it though? What did he mean?"

I could see the puzzled expressions on everybody's faces. What on earth was she talking about? The character had said what he meant, hadn't he? Another minute of silence passed, with only the occasional sound of pages slowly being turned. I looked up to see Rachel turn to Alyssa and shrug. I went to the page where Atticus told Jem it was a sin to kill a mockingbird, hoping to find the answer to why he had said that. I kept reading along until I found an explanation from Miss Maudie, the housekeeper. "Your father's right," she said. "Mockingbirds don't eat up people's gardens, don't nest in corncribs, they don't do one thing but sing their hearts out for us. That's why it's a sin to kill a mockingbird" (Lee).

Mrs. Hart turned in my direction. "Lacy, you look like you found something," she said.

"Yeah, the housekeeper tells the kids that it's a sin to kill a mockingbird because they are good; they don't do anything but sing their hearts out for us."

"Good," Mrs. Hart replied. "Mockingbirds are good; they don't cause problems. In fact, they are the ones that start the singing. They will sing, and the other birds will follow."

"So why would anyone want to kill them then, if they don't bother anyone, not even other birds?" queried Kate.

"Ah, that is the real question," said Mrs. Hart. "Why would anyone want to harm something or someone who is innocent? Wouldn't you all agree that the mockingbird is innocent?"

"Well, that's just awful!" cried Amanda indignantly. "How terrible to want to hurt something beautiful that is sharing its lovely song with the world!"

"That's so unfair!" chimed in Alyssa. "The mockingbird doesn't do anything wrong. No one should be allowed to hurt it."

"Okay, so you all think that it is wrong to kill a mockingbird. Does Jem shoot a mockingbird with his pellet gun? Is bird hunting the main theme of the story?" asked Mrs. Hart.

Everyone looked around, confused. We had just figured it out, hadn't we? Why was Mrs. Hart asking us another question. Seeing that we didn't understand what she was asking, Mrs. Hart tried again. "What is the main idea of the story?"

I raised my hand. "It's the story of Jem and Scout growing up in the South."

Mrs. Hart nodded. "Yes, now give me more details. Let's make a chart. I want you all to copy this into your notebook and then finish filling it in for homework."

Event	Characters	Who Is Innocent	Who Is Not Innocent, the Wrongdoer
Presents left in the tree	Boo Radley, Jem and Scout	Jem and Scout	

After she had written the chart on the board, Rachel raised her hand. "Mrs. Hart, should we put Boo Radley in the Not Innocent column? You didn't write his name down."

"That's a good question, Rachel. What do you think? Did Boo Radley do anything wrong by leaving the gifts in the tree for them?"

"No," answered Rachel, slowly as if unsure.

"No, he didn't doing anything wrong."

"So would we write his name in the Innocent category then?" pursued Rachel.

"Yes. If he didn't do anything wrong, that would make him innocent, wouldn't it?" asked Mrs. Hart, looking around the room. "Okay, so add Boo's name to the innocent column for the first example, then fill the chart in with two more examples from the story."

"But then the Wrongdoer column is blank," said Aimee with a questioning tone. "Can we leave that blank?"

"If there is no one who has done something wrong, I believe that it does have to be blank," stated Mrs. Hart.

That evening, I filled in the rest of the chart for homework. It was pretty easy. I just thought of a couple of the main events from the story and filled in the blanks. Mrs. Hart said to add two more examples, but I couldn't help think that the mockingbird should be in the chart somewhere too, so I added it to the bottom.

Event	Characters	Who Is Innocent	Who Is Not Innocent, the Wrongdoer
Presents left in the tree	Boo Radley, Jem, and Scout	Jem and Scout and Boo Radley	
Scout and Jem attacked on way home from pageant	Jem, Scout, attacker (Mr. Ewell), rescuer (Boo Radley)	Jem, Scout, Boo Radley	Mr. Ewell
Tom Robinson's trial	Tom Robinson, Atticus (Jem's dad, lawyer), Ms. Ewell, Mr. Ewell	Tom Robinson, Atticus	Mr. Ewell
Jem's pellet gun	Jem, Scout, Atticus, housekeeper, mockingbird	Jem, Scout, Atticus, housekeeper, mockingbird	

I finished my other homework, but I kept thinking about the chart. I took out my English binder to look at it again. I realized that there was no wrongdoer written in for the pellet gun entry; maybe that was what was bothering me. No, that couldn't be it. Mrs. Hart said that was okay to leave it blank if there was no wrongdoer. I looked again at the chart, and instead of reading across, I read down the columns. Jem and Scout were always listed in the Innocent column, but so was Boo Radley! How could Boo be innocent? No one liked Boo; everyone was afraid of him. I thought about the story again. Were people afraid of him because he was mean or loud or nasty? Had he done mean things to anyone? I could not think of a single thing. Looking back at the chart, I realized that it was just the opposite. Boo was always kind, considerate, and quiet. Then it really hit me. People aren't always the way you imagine them to be. Boo Radley was no monster; he was a caring human being! He even saved Scout and Jem the night of the pageant when they were attacked by Mr. Ewell on their way home.

I whirled around in my chair as I felt a light tap on my shoulder. I jumped and screamed in surprise. It was Jade! I was so engrossed in my thoughts that I hadn't even heard her knock and come in.

"Hey, I didn't mean to scare you!" Jade laughed as she plunked down on the edge of my bed. "What are you doing that you didn't even notice me?"

"Oh nothing much, just looking over my homework. We're reading *To Kill a Mockingbird*."

"Uh huh, we are too. What's your homework?"

"Mrs. Hart had us make a chart. Do you want to see?"

"Sure. Why not?" answered Jade. She looked at it for a minute, then asked, "Why are there blanks? Aren't you finished?"

"Oh, that's okay. Mrs. Hart said we could leave them empty if there's no wrongdoer for that part."

Then I saw light come up in Jade's eyes as a smile spread across her face. "Now I get why that's the title of the book!" she said excitedly.

"What do you mean?"

"Look at who's in the Innocent column!" she said, pointing.

"So what? Of course Jem and Scout are innocent. You didn't expect their dad or the housekeeper to be evil either, did you?" I answered.

"No, silly. Who else is in that column?"

It was almost as if she could read my mind. It was what I was thinking before she showed up. We looked right at each other and said at the exact same moment, "Boo Radley!"

"Jade, that's what I was thinking a few minutes ago. Boo is not the bad guy in the story. He is not the monster that people make him out to be."

"Right. And who else is listed as innocent?" she persisted.

I looked at the chart again. "Tom Robinson and—oh! The mockingbird! The mockingbird is innocent! Of course, Boo and Tom are mockingbirds who never hurt anybody. They are the innocent victims." I looked away as I added, "Just like Faith," in a low voice.

Jade was nodding in agreement. "Yeah, I guess you could call Faith a mockingbird," she said slowly as her expression of glee changed to one of sorrow.

We sat there staring emptily into space for a couple of minutes as the weight of that realization sunk in.

I took my pen and added a few more rows to my chart.

Event	Characters	Who Is Innocent	Who Is Not Innocent, the Wrongdoer
Presents left in the tree	Boo Radley, Jem, and Scout	Jem and Scout and Boo Radley	
Scout and Jem attacked on way home from pageant	Jem, Scout, attacker (Mr. Ewell), rescuer (Boo Radley)	Jem, Scout, Boo Radley	Mr. Ewell
Tom Robinson's trial	Tom Robinson, Atticus (Jem's dad, lawyer), Ms. Ewell, Mr. Ewell	Tom Robinson, Atticus	Mr. Ewell
Jem's pellet gun	Jem, Scout, Atticus, housekeeper, mockingbird	Jem, Scout, Atticus, housekeeper, mockingbird	

Faith defends me in class, calls out the other girls for being mean	Faith, me, rest of girls in class	Faith, me	Girls in our class
Faith being bullied at lunch	Faith, me, Alyssa, Rachel	Faith, me	Alyssa and Rachel
Faith accused of vandalism	Faith, Mrs. Strickland, Kate, anonymous witnesses	Faith	Anonymous witnesses who spread rumor, real vandal (who are they?)

I finished writing and looked somberly over at Jade. "Faith is definitely in the innocent column, but how do we find out who the witnesses and the real vandal are?" I asked, exasperated. "Too bad that this isn't a book and we could just skip to the end and find out," I groaned.

"Ha-ha, that would be great, wouldn't it? If it weren't even real?"

Toward the end of English class the next day, we discussed the novel some more. Mrs. Hart had us take out our chart, and we filled in the blank template on the board with our answers. Pretty much everyone wrote down the same examples from the story that I did. Then we talked about how Boo Radley was really a nice person who was just misunderstood. Then Mrs. Hart asked us another question.

"Think about your life and the people you know," she began. "Can you think of any innocent victims, mockingbirds, who have been hurt needlessly by others?"

The room went completely silent, and I felt my brain explode. I didn't dare turn to look at the others, but I swear I could feel their eyes like sharp daggers piercing my back. Why? Why did she have to ask that question? Did she see the rest of my chart? No, that was impossible. I had my arm covering it the whole class.

Mrs. Hart waited a couple of long moments and then continued.

"What about in the Bible? Are there any examples of innocent victims in the Bible?"

Huh? That idea hadn't occurred to me before; there must have been. I tried to quickly remember the Bible stories, but one name, Faith, kept running through my head. I couldn't look up. If I looked up, then she would call on me, I reasoned nervously. Then I heard Aimee saying something.

"What was that, Aimee?" asked Mrs. Hart. "Please speak loudly so that everyone can hear the answer this time."

"Jesus. Jesus was crucified, and he hadn't done anything wrong." I gulped.

Yes, of course, Jesus was the best answer. Now that it was safe, I looked up to see Mrs. Hart adding another row to the chart.

"Please add this row to your chart before the bell rings," she instructed. "We can discuss this aspect more tomorrow."

Just as she finished the row, the bell rang, and Kate called out, "Do you want our homework?" which elicited a response of "Yes, just leave it on my desk."

Event	Characters	Who Is Innocent	Who Is Not Innocent, the Wrongdoer
Presents left in the tree	Boo Radley, Jem, and Scout	Jem and Scout and Boo Radley	
Scout and Jem attacked on way home from pageant	Jem, Scout, attacker (Mr. Ewell), rescuer (Boo Radley)	Jem, Scout, Boo Radley	Mr. Ewell
Tom Robinson's trial	Tom Robinson, Atticus (Jem's dad, lawyer), Ms. Ewell, Mr. Ewell	Tom Robinson, Atticus	Mr. Ewell

Jem's pellet gun	Jem, Scout, Atticus, housekeeper, mockingbird	Jem, Scout, Atticus, housekeeper, mockingbird	
Faith defends me in class, calls out the other girls for being mean	Faith, me, rest of girls in class	Faith, me	Girls in our class
Faith being bullied at lunch	Faith, me, Alyssa, Rachel	Faith, me	Alyssa and Rachel
Faith accused of vandalism	Faith, Mrs. Strickland, Kate, anonymous witnesses	Faith	Anonymous witnesses who spread rumor, real vandal (who are they?)
Jesus's crucifixion	Jesus, Jews, Pharisees / Pontius Pilot / disciples	Jesus, the Lamb of God	Jews, Pharisees, Pontius Pilot, Judas Iscariot (disciple) who betrayed him, disciples (Peter who denied Jesus)

I hurriedly finished copying the row and began to tear the page out of my binder to pass in when I realized that I still had the extra rows in my chart.

Panicking, I quickly went over to Mrs. Hart. "Could I please rewrite my homework and give it to you later? I didn't know you were collecting this, and it is so messy."

Mrs. Hart glanced over at my homework, took it, and answered cheerily, "No, it's fine. It's not messy at all. I can read it. Have a good day!"

And with that, I was dismissed from class. Even though Mrs. Hart said my homework was fine, somehow I knew that wouldn't be the last word on it. The day dragged on. Every other minute, I found myself thinking about that homework and wondering if Mrs. Hart had looked at mine yet. What would she do when she read it? Would she be mad at me? Would she call my mom? What if she showed it to Mrs. Strickland or the principal? Oh! Why did I add those rows about Faith? I moaned inwardly.

I arrived at school the next day, just going through the motions, waiting for the bomb to drop. I walked past Mrs. Hart in the hall, but she seemed not to notice me. I gathered my books for class and tried to forget about the homework and what the consequences might be. I wished I had a friend close by, a confidante with whom I could share my nervousness. Just as I was thinking that, I felt my phone vibrate. It was Jade. "No worries. You got this." I smiled when I saw her text. It was like she could read my mind. I guess we were still twinsies; she could always tell when I needed encouragement. When I walked into English class, I noticed that Mrs. Hart had the chart from yesterday up on the whiteboard. Everyone took their seats, and Mrs. Hart handed back our homework. I was on the edge of my seat, waiting to see if she had said anything about what I wrote about Faith. Much to my surprise and relief, there was just a big red checkmark acknowledging that I had done the work. I began to relax as Mrs. Hart started the lesson.

"Ladies, all of you did a great job making and filling in the chart. You all are beginning to understand the underlying point of the story." We all smiled, happy to be complimented.

Mrs. Hart continued, "In fact, I liked your answers so much I intentionally left blank rows on this chart"—she pointed—"so that you could share them today with the class." The smiles changed to looks of dismay as Mrs. Hart was passing out the dry-erase markers. No one wanted to write their answer on the board. I quickly put my head down and began taking notes. Hopefully she wouldn't notice me. I began to earnestly pray that I wouldn't get a marker, that she would forget about me. How could I possibly write mine about Faith up there for all of *them* to see? Aimee and Rachel went first. Aimee wrote about her sister getting blamed for not cleaning their room. Rachel's was funny. She wrote about her dog getting blamed for getting into the garbage, but they later realized that it was a raccoon! A couple of other people went up, and then it was my turn.

I couldn't think of anything cute or funny that I could write. I went up to the board with my stomach churning and my heart racing. Everyone would be mad at me, but I couldn't think of anything else to write. I had to write about Faith. My hand shook as I filled in the chart.

Faith defends me in class, calls out the other girls for being mean	Faith, me, rest of girls in class	Faith, me	Girls in our class

I turned to go back to my seat when I heard Mrs. Hart say, "Lacy, that is a good one, but would you please also put the other one that you wrote down for homework." I hesitated, and she gave me an encouraging nod. I shuffled back up to the board and wrote the next row:

Faith being bullied at lunch	Faith, me, Alyssa, Rachel	Faith, me	Alyssa and Rachel

I quickly sat back down and began fixing the things in my backpack, not wanting to look at the other girls. Everyone had been chatting with their friends while we took turns up at the board. Suddenly though, the room went completely silent.

Then I heard Rachel react, calling out loudly, "What! No way!"

Alyssa chimed in, "That is so bogus!"

The noise level began to grow as they protested their names being on the board as wrongdoers. Mrs. Hart put her hands up to ask for quiet.

"Okay, okay. Let's talk about some of the answers on the board. We'll start with Lacy's since hers seems to be the most provocative."

Rachel yelled, "That's wrong! She's just being mean!"

Alyssa nodded her head in agreement. I shrank down into my seat. I wanted to be invisible. Mrs. Hart looked over at me.

"Lacy, since it is your answer, you will start the discussion. Tell us the background situation that explains the information in the chart."

I looked around uncomfortably at the pinched faces and menacing stares. *Oh, Lord!* I thought. *Why do I have to do this? Please help me!*

Although I was scared, I recounted what happened that day, my voice trembling as I described how the gang had taken Faith's lunch and hidden it from her.

Alyssa tried to interrupt, but Mrs. Hart stopped her, saying, "After Lacy has finished, you may comment on this example."

Alyssa sat silently and pouted as I told how I felt badly that Faith had no lunch and shared mine with her at the other table.

Before Alyssa could interject again, Kate blurted out half-laughing, "I remember that day. You were sitting on Faith's lunch bag, Alyssa."

"Yeah," added Aimee. "It was funny when she couldn't find it."

"That's because Alyssa has a big bottom!" said Rachel with a grin, making everyone laugh.

Alyssa looked angrily from face to face and said through clenched teeth, "We weren't bullying her. We were only joking around!"

Mrs. Hart waited a few seconds and then asked, "Who here would like it if somebody took their lunch and wouldn't give it back?"

Nobody raised their hand. She continued. "Okay, no one. Who wants someone to sit on their lunch?"

Again, no one raised their hand. "I guess it was kind of a mean thing to do," mumbled Laura. They all turned to look at Alyssa.

"Don't look at me! It was Rachel's idea!" Alyssa practically spat out the words.

Mrs. Hart looked at all of us, saying calmly but with purpose in her voice, "I believe that we should all make the effort to care about others. Put yourself in the other person's shoes. If someone were doing or saying that thing to you, how would you feel?" Alyssa and Rachel hung their heads a little. No one said a word. "For class tomorrow, read the next three pages," instructed Mrs. Hart before the bell rang.

After we were a few feet from the classroom and almost to our lockers, I heard Alyssa and Rachel walking behind me, complaining loudly.

"Lacy is such a witch! I can't believe that she said we were bullying Faith!"

"I know!" agreed Rachel. "Some people just can't take a joke. I mean we gave her her lunch back."

"Now we're probably going to get a detention or something," groused

Alyssa. "It's all Lacy's fault. Why couldn't she just keep her mouth shut? We didn't hurt anyone."

"Yeah." Rachel nodded. "It's not like it was a big deal."

At that comment, I whirled around to face them. "Can you two think of anyone but yourselves?" I yelled.

Rachel sneered. "Oh look, it's little Miss Goody Two-shoes." Alyssa laughed snidely.

I would not get flustered. I would not let them bully me this time. I stood in front of them, waiting for an answer to my question.

"Move," commanded Alyssa. "I'm trying to get to my locker."

I repeated my question, trying not to let my voice shake. I was determined not to move until I got an answer.

"She said move!" said Rachel as she gave me a little shove.

By this time, the other students were noticing that something was going on. They were stopping to watch and listen. The crowd began to murmur when Rachel shoved me.

"No," I answered firmly. "Answer my question. Don't you ever think of anyone else? I guess not, since you thought it was *fun* to hurt Faith," I said bitingly.

Alyssa's jaw dropped in surprise, but she recovered quickly. "Oh! Little Miss Goody Two-shoes thinks she's tough!" she taunted.

The group of students was forming a circle around us, and I could hear them murmuring, "Fight! Fight!" A fight—that was the last thing I needed or wanted. I didn't need to get expelled from school like Faith! I looked around at the crowd, my blood boiling, my back as straight and stiff as a metal pole. I was so angry at Alyssa and Rachel. I really did want to wipe those snide smiles off of their faces. That's when I noticed that my fists were clenched. I shifted from foot to foot, trying to think of what to say next when suddenly there was a familiar voice.

"No!"

I turned to see Kyle push his way through the crowd. He stood in front of me, facing Alyssa and Rachel.

"Why don't you just answer her question?" he challenged, staring them down.

An ally! I had an ally! I wasn't in this by myself after all! Everyone stood there waiting for their response.

After a few seconds, I could hear other voices. "Answer the question!" "Yeah, just answer it!" and then another "Why were you bullying Faith?" It was Kate.

It got quiet again as Kate came to stand in front of Rachel. "Why did you do it? Why did you bully Faith?"

Alyssa and Rachel looked around with wide eyes but still tried to keep up appearances.

"What? You know that it was just a joke," Alyssa replied, trying to pass it off.

"No, no it wasn't," I answered firmly. "You were being mean, and you knew it. You know it now too."

The warning bell for class rang. Kyle took my arm, saying, "Let's go," and led me away through the crowd.

"Lacy, sorry."

"Sorry?" I asked, confused. "Why should you be saying sorry when I should be thanking you? Kyle, that was great! Thank you for helping me out of a jam there."

"It was the least I could do after …" Kyle's voice trailed off, and he didn't finish his thought, not out loud at least.

"No, really, thank you. If you didn't step in, it could've turned into a fight."

"Aw, it was nothing. You're the brave one, not me."

"What do you mean?"

"The way you stood up for Faith. That was awesome."

We were almost to the classroom when Kyle stopped and looked straight into my eyes. "Lacy, I'm sorry. I'm sorry I thought you ratted out Faith. Everyone was saying it. Can you forgive me?"

"I … I …" I didn't know what to say. How could he have believed I would do that? I could feel the sadness creep into my soul and my smile droop to a frown.

The warning bell rang. Kyle gave me a quick side hug and said again, "Sorry," as he left for his class. Then he turned and mouthed the words "Talk to you later" before hurrying off.

I entered class, my thoughts and emotions awhirl. Kyle had defended me. Kyle had taken my hand and even hugged me! I should have been ecstatic, but I wasn't. He had thought that I had betrayed Faith. I knew that a lot of people thought I had told on her, but Kyle! I wanted so badly to believe that he knew me better than that—that I wouldn't do that to a friend. I thought he cared about me! I wished I could just go sit by myself and have a good cry. *Why, oh why would he believe that I would do that?* I wondered. I could not cry. I *would* not cry there, not then. Alyssa and Rachel were still grumbling to each other on the other side of the room. I definitely would not cry in front of them. They would enjoy it too much.

I was glad that it was math class; there wouldn't be any discussions about emotions or feelings. Mr. Grimes only spoke in concrete mathematical terms. As long as I kept my eyes on the board or my paper, I could get through the hour. Then I would have some alone time to sort out my feelings at lunch.

Finally it was lunchtime. I left class, secretly hoping to see Kyle coming to meet me. I stood by the doorway a few seconds before deciding that I looked dumb waiting for someone who wasn't coming. I plastered a smile on my face and walked briskly to my locker. Maybe Kyle would be there with his back against the lockers, like guys did when they wanted to look macho. I turned the corner, and my heart sank. He was there, but he was talking to Aimee, Kate, and Alyssa. Why was he talking with them? I could feel my hands turn into fists and my jaw tighten. I quickened my pace and walked past them to the restroom. *Brave? Hah! What a laugh!* I couldn't even go to my own locker when he was there. They were all probably laughing about me acting like I was tough. Except I hadn't been acting earlier. I was so angry with them for bullying Faith that I had forgotten to be afraid. *Is that bravery?* I asked myself as I washed my hands and brushed my hair.

I entered the lunchroom and took my usual seat at the table behind the gang. As I ate, I doodled in my notebook, lost in my thoughts. "Hey, is that a picture of me?" a cheery voice asked as he plopped down on the bench next to me. I turned to see Kyle and his sparking blue eyes smiling at me. My heart leapt as a smile spread across my face.

"Uh, no. It's a teddy bear, see?" I said, pushing the book over to him.

"Yeah, it's good. I was only kidding. I knew it wasn't me." We sat there looking at each other, saying nothing. Why didn't he say something? Why did he come over if he had nothing to say?

"So, uh, Lacy, do you forgive me?"

"Forgive you? Oh, I don't know. I guess so," I mumbled.

"No you don't."

"Yeah … yeah …"

"No, you don't," he answered resolutely. "And I don't blame you."

"Well … I …"

"I couldn't help it though. What was I supposed to think? One day, we're all at your house, and then the next day it seems you're not talking to Faith."

"Huh? What?"

"Yeah. Did you guys have a fight or something?"

"No … no …"

"It was just weird—you know? She was talking to me, telling me how mean the other girls are but how nice you are. Then you two weren't talking anymore. I felt so bad for her. She cried, saying that you were just like them." He paused a minute after that last bit, waiting for my reaction.

I was flabbergasted! Me, just like *them*! I almost sprayed the water I was drinking all over the table, but I managed to gulp it down without choking.

He continued, "So when everybody was saying that you got her kicked out, I mean, I didn't want to believe it, but it seemed reasonable. It made me wonder if it wasn't true that Jade and Marie left because you didn't really get along with them either."

My heart practically stopped when he mentioned Jade and Marie. Why was he telling me that? Was that what everybody was saying, that I was a witch, that I had no friends because I drove them away? I felt like the whole cafeteria was watching us, staring at me. Was this whole thing another *joke*? Did Alyssa set this up so they could make fun of me?

"Lacy? You okay? You're really quiet," Kyle said softly. I expected to see him smirking, but there was a look of concern on his furrowed brow instead. Out of the corner of my eye, I could see Rachel and the other girls looking over at us, waiting to see what was going to happen. I wanted to yell, to scream, to cry, but mostly I wanted to run—run right out of that room and keep on running. I wanted to get away from Kyle, from them … from myself.

"No, Dakota, I didn't answer him." I had just finished explaining to Dakota what Kyle had told me.

"Why not?" she texted back. Why not? What kind of a question was that! I couldn't make a scene in front of the whole lunchroom. Duh! Besides, how could I tell him that it really was my fault that Jade and Marie left our school, but that it was really complicated. If I said that, he would think I had been a lousy friend who would probably rat out Faith too.

"Why? What was I supposed to say?" I shot back.

Not a minute later, my phone buzzed. "The truth."

The truth. But that was so complicated. No one wanted to hear the truth. It was messy and inconvenient, and no one wanted to sit quietly for long enough to hear it all. I was sure that he would just cut my explanation short, walk away, or turn off his phone.

"No one wants to hear that. Besides, it's too long," I texted back.

"What do you mean no one?" she asked. "I listened."

That was true, but Dakota was my sister. "That's different. You're my sister," I responded.

"Lacy, you want them to give you a chance, don't you? So you have to give them a chance. You can't just shut people out."

As I read her words, I knew it was true but also really scary. I was tired of putting myself out there just so I could be reminded how much I didn't fit in.

"Dakota, you make it sound easy, but it isn't," I texted back.

"I know, but you don't want to be alone, do you?" she asked.

Her question made me uncomfortable. Sometimes I hated being alone, or rather being reminded that I had no friends at school. Being alone actually wasn't so bad. I liked having quiet time to think and daydream, and I didn't miss hanging around with fake people—if that was what she meant.

"IDK being alone can be nice ..."

"Seriously? Don't you get lonely?"

Lonely. Was I lonely? I wondered. I texted back: "Not usually. I talk to you and Jade and Marie after school."

"That's good, but it's not the same as having a friend at school to hang out with."

Of course I knew she was right. I missed Faith. "That's why I need to help clear Faith's name. Any ideas?"

"You found the letters, right?"

"Yup."

"Well, then check your evidence," Dakota answered. "Tell me what you figure out. TTYL."

I went to retrieve the notes I had from Alyssa, Rachel, Faith, and Kyle. I wished that Marie had kept the note last year when the gang bullied her. It would have been a big help toward showing who the real culprits were. I read the notes over and over again but didn't see how they could prove Faith's innocence. Feeling frustrated and angry, I looked over at my clock and realized that it was getting late, and I still had homework to do for tomorrow. I put the notes and the pictures of the graffiti back into the desk drawer and prayed that somehow everything would work out and the truth would prevail. "Please, Lord, I know that you are there and you hear and see everything. You know that Faith is innocent. Please, please help me find the answer! Please help me prove to everyone that Faith didn't vandalize the school." As I finished praying, a tear rolled down my face, but as I reached for a tissue, I felt that a huge weight had been lifted off of my shoulders.

The date of the science fair kept edging closer. Mrs. Strickland had informed us that we should be working on the experiment portion of our project. I found the rough draft of my research paper and the writing samples that I had already gathered. Mostly, I only had samples from the girls in my class. I still needed to ask more people so that I had a large enough sample pool of participants. Well, I could begin classifying the samples I already had, couldn't I? Then I could at least have the data tables set up and a few entries done for class tomorrow. Mrs. Strickland had made it very clear that she would be checking our notebooks tomorrow. I started by grouping the samples into stacks of right-handedness and left-handedness. Not surprisingly, there were three times as many samples for people who wrote with their right hand. So far, only Aimee, Kate, and Alyssa were lefties. I looked at the samples from the lefties first since there were fewer of them. It was cool how their writing always seemed to be on a slant instead of straight up and down. It made their writing look elegant—even Alyssa's, which was written in thick marker. Slanted writing in thick black marker … Somehow it looked familiar. Where had I seen it before? I wasn't friends with Alyssa. She never passed notes to *me*, or *did* she? On impulse, I reached for the mean note that I had gotten from the gang. It was the awful picture of me running away from the volleyball. There were no words on it, but the drawing was scribbled in black marker. What about the note Faith got in her locker? I picked that one up to inspect it. It was written in black marker too. I looked at it again, trying to see if there was a slant to the letters. No, they were definitely straight up and down, so it had not been written by a lefty. I decided to look at Faith's note to Kyle too. Not surprisingly, it was written in pen, and even though I just had a copy now, I remembered that the original note was written in purple ink. *Hey, I should check that Faith's handwriting in the note doesn't look like the handwriting in the girls' restroom*, I thought. Excitedly, I took out my phone so that I could compare the pictures I took to the copy of the note. Everything about the two samples of handwriting were different. Faith's handwriting was small, delicate, and meticulous. All the letters were the proper height, all i's dotted and t's crossed. The writing from the bathroom looked like a huge scribble, hurried looking and messily written with thick black marker. It was difficult to distinguish between o's and a's and e's and i's. This was definitely not the same person's handwriting. My gaze shifted from one to the other. The writing from the bathroom was even slanted, while Faith's writing was as straight and tall as a soldier. *Wait a minute! The graffiti was slanted!* That meant that someone left-handed must have written it! I looked back at the samples I had from lefties: Aimee, Kate, and Alyssa. *That's right! Alyssa is a lefty … and she likes to write in black marker—chunky black marker! It must have been her that vandalized the restroom! Did she write the horrible note to Faith too?* I grabbed the note to compare it to the graffiti. It was also written in black marker, but it looked totally different. The handwriting, though hurried, was still easy to read. The lettering was nearly perfect and actually graceful, almost beautiful. I looked from one to the other again and noticed that the marker used in the note was not thick, and the writing wasn't slanted either. Nope, these were definitely written by two different people. The person who wrote the note was most likely right-handed.

I had it! I really had it! Dakota was right. The letters *were* the evidence that Faith did not vandalize the restroom. I was so happy that I began to sing and dance around the room. Woohoo! Now that I could prove it wasn't Faith, she could come back to school. I had to tell Jade! Even though it was late, I was sure she wouldn't mind if I texted her now.

"I solved it!" I typed.

Buzz-buzz. She was still awake. "What?"

"I have the proof."

"Huh?"

Well, maybe she wasn't as awake as I'd thought. "Jade, I can prove it wasn't Faith."

A minute or two passed. Then my phone buzzed again. "Wow! Really?"

"Yeah, the letters prove it wasn't her!"

I waited a few more minutes but got no response. She must have fallen asleep. I'd just have to fill her in on the details tomorrow. It was getting late, but I was so excited I knew that I wouldn't be able to fall asleep. I was giddy with the knowledge that I could save Faith and redeem my reputation. *Dakota! I should let her know the good news!*

"Dakota, you were right!" I texted.

A few seconds later, my phone buzzed "Of course. About what?"

"The letters. I found them, and they aren't Faith's handwriting."

"Awesome! So have you shown the principal yet?" she asked.

Shown the principal … I was so excited about having solved the problem that I hadn't realized I hadn't finished solving the actual problem. I would have to go talk to the principal and show him the letters. What would he say? What would his reaction be? Would he even listen to me? I could feel my euphoria fade as reality set back in. I hated talking to people I didn't know very well. Other people would say that I was shy, but it was more of an anxiety attack in the moment. I so badly wanted everything to go right and for people to like me that I was scared to say the wrong thing. Instead, I broke out into a sweat and stammered as if my tongue was wrapped around my tonsils. *Oh why! Why do I have to be the one to go tell the principal?* I began to be filled with a sense of dread.

"Lacy, what's wrong? Are you there?" asked Dakota.

I looked over at my clock. I must have phased out thinking about confronting the principal. It had been a few minutes since she had texted me about talking to him.

"Yeah. I'm here."

"What's the matter?" she asked again.

"You know I don't like talking to people, especially grown-ups."

"So? You're gonna chicken out?"

No! No … I couldn't do that! Faith was relying on me. I had to bring the truth out into the light. I was her only chance at being vindicated.

"Lacy?"

"Oh, yeah. I mean, no! I have to clear Faith's name." *And my own*, I thought.

"Good! So you'll go see the principal tomorrow."

Tomorrow? I gulped. *Tomorrow is so close. I don't feel ready to explain the whole situation to the principal.* "Can't I wait a day or two?" I responded, feeling sheepish.

"No way! You need to get this straightened out ASAP!"

I could feel myself being torn in two by the conflict between logic and emotion. I knew that I should talk with him, but I was afraid.

"Lacy? R U still there?"

"Yup."

"Maybe ask Mom to go with you …"

"I'll have to finish explaining the whole thing to her."

"So? Better now than later."

Dakota was right. The principal, Pastor Dave, would probably want to talk to an adult anyway. It would be better for Mom to know what was going on before he called her. "Okay, I'll tell her in the morning. Everyone is already asleep."

"Okay, night."

"Thanks, sis."

"No prob."

I woke up to the sound of Sticky barking madly and my mother yelling. The sunlight was already streaming into my room through the open shade. Confused, I looked over at the clock on my dresser, 7:40. No way! I'd have enough time to throw some clothes on and go. There was definitely no time to braid my hair like I wanted to do. I got dressed and practically flew down the stairs.

"Mom, I'm ready! Let's go!" I called out.

My dad's voice bellowed from the living room "She's already out there!" I grabbed my backpack and sprinted to the car.

"Why are you so late today?" asked Mom as I plopped down into the passenger seat.

"Uh, I guess I forgot to set my alarm," I answered, still trying to fasten my seat belt.

Mom turned out of the driveway onto the street. "So, why were you up so late?"

The question surprised me. Hadn't they already been asleep when I went to bed?

When I didn't answer, Mom waited a moment and then prompted me, saying, "I'm waiting," in that terse tone she used when she wanted me to know it was a serious conversation.

"I, uh …"

"And don't tell me that you were doing homework," she cautioned, glancing toward me.

But I had been doing my homework! I thought, so I blurted out, "I was working on my science project."

"Oh, I didn't realize your project required singing and dancing at midnight," came the quick reply.

"Oh no! I didn't wake you up, did I?" I asked, suddenly sorry for how much noise I'd made. "I was just so happy that I can help Faith."

"Help Faith?" asked Mom quizzically. "But wasn't she expelled?"

"Yeah, but when I was looking at the data for my science project, I noticed that it couldn't have possibly been Faith who wrote the graffiti."

"What do you mean?" asked Mom as she turned into the school parking lot.

"Well, you know that my project is about handedness, so I was going over the handwriting samples I have."

"So? How can that prove that Faith is innocent?" prodded Mom.

"I took a picture of the graffiti in the restroom the day it happened,

Mom. I also have a sample of Faith's handwriting. You know what? They don't match—at all! It's not even close, Mom. They are totally different styles, and it even looks like the graffiti was written by someone left-handed! It so definitely wasn't Faith."

Mom stopped the car and turned to stare at me, her lips pursed and eyebrows furrowed.

"Lacy, now that you have proof, what are you going to do?"

"What *am* I going to do?" a little voice inside me whispered. "Well … Dakota thinks I should talk to you and then tell the principal," I answered slowly, not looking at Mom.

"I don't know, Lacy," Mom started. "You don't want to get in trouble too."

Suddenly I could feel an inner voice explode inside of me, and without thinking, I yelled,

"No! I won't let it happen! Not again!"

"Lacy, calm down. What are you talking about?"

"Mom, I lost all my friends because I was a coward and didn't help them! I need to stand up for what is right. I need to tell the truth!" I slammed the car door shut and marched through the double doors into the school building, not waiting for my mother's reaction.

As I went down the hallway, I began to notice that everyone was quietly staring at me as I walked past. It was eerie; the hallway was never that quiet during school hours. My usual insecurities came flooding back. Was my hair a mess? Did my outfit look hideous? Did I look that awful without makeup? I felt like I had *loser* stamped across my forehead. I was almost to my locker when I felt a tap on the shoulder "Hey, Lacy, everything okay?"

It was Kyle! Still feeling angry after the conversation with Mom, I didn't dare open my mouth, not wanting to yell at him too. Instead, I forced a weak smile and nodded.

"Are you sure? I heard you yelling when you got out of the car, and you look ready to pummel someone."

Oh! So that must be why everyone is staring! I looked down to see that my fists were clenched.

"Lacy, are you grinding your teeth?" asked Kyle with concern in his voice.

He was right. My jaw was tight, and I must have looked like I was growling. I tried to laugh it off.

"Yeah, heh-heh. I guess I'm a little stressed," I answered as I turned toward my locker to put my books away.

As the warning bell began to ring, Kyle leaned closer to whisper in my ear, "Let me know if you want to talk," before sprinting to his first class. It was like magic! Kyle's sweet words and kind eyes melted away my anger, and his warm breath brushing past my ear gave me goose bumps. I didn't care anymore who was staring at me. I was happy! I floated into class on a cloud of love and joy. Maybe I *could* confide in Kyle about finding the evidence to prove Faith's innocence. Then he would know that I wasn't the one who got her expelled. Hopefully we would sit together at lunch again.

I decided to make sure to bump into Kyle between classes to suggest it. All I had to say was that I needed to talk; he would understand. As soon as the bell rang, I made a beeline to the hallway by his locker. I saw him leaving class talking to Caleb, who looked angry. Whoa! I *did not* want to get more involved in that noise. As far as I knew, Caleb still blamed me for Faith being expelled. I turned around, hoping they hadn't seen me, when I felt a hand on my shoulder.

"Lacy, Lacy … wait up." It was Kyle. "Did you want to talk?"

Caleb was right behind Kyle, glaring at me. I just nodded, afraid to speak.

"Okay," Kyle answered, looking from my face to Caleb's. "How about lunch?"

I nodded in agreement, then hurried off to my next class, praying that Caleb wouldn't be a part of our lunch table.

English class was quieter than usual since we were taking a test. So it was really obvious when my phone began to ping. The first time or two, everybody ignored it. But then it kept on going off! It sounded like a firecracker exploding! I was so embarrassed. The whole class was looking at me, and Mrs. Hart was not amused either.

"Lacy, you know that you are not supposed to have your phone in class."

"I know, but I wasn't using it. I'll turn it off right now."

I fumbled for my backpack where I had put it. *Ping. Ping. Ping.* It never failed. Whenever I got nervous and tried to do something quickly, my hands wouldn't cooperate. Mrs. Hart was walking toward me just as I got the backpack unzipped. *Ping. Ping. Ping.* She had a scowl on her face. I braced myself. Was she going to take my phone away?

"Lacy, this is very disruptive for everyone. If you can't turn it off quickly, I will have to confiscate it."

Beads of sweat were forming on my forehead as I groped around in my bag for the phone. After what seemed like a century, I pulled it out. *Ping. Ping.* It was Jade. She probably wanted to talk about the evidence. How I wished I could look at her texts! I had to turn my phone off, though, if I wanted to keep it. *Sorry, Jade,* I thought. *It will have to wait at least until lunch or maybe even after school.*

I got to the lunchroom and looked around. Everything was the same. The gang was sitting in their usual seats. The teachers were chatting nonchalantly at their table. The guys were goofing around, balancing cheese on their noses and punting cherry tomatoes through pretzel goal posts. I didn't see Kyle, so I sat dejectedly in my usual seat. I felt like a fool for having thought things would be different. Where was Kyle anyway? He was the one who had suggested lunch. I took a bite out of my sandwich and stared straight ahead at the wall. I couldn't stand to watch Rachel, Alyssa, and Aimee snickering at me as I sat all alone. Lunch was almost over when I felt someone slide in on the bench next to me.

"Sorry I'm late."

Late? Boy, that was an understatement. There was only five minutes of lunch left. I looked over at Kyle dispiritedly.

"Lacy, really, it wasn't my fault," Kyle tried to explain. "Caleb—" But then the bell rang, and all I could do was watch his lips move, like in one of those old soundless movies. I shrugged, gathered my things, and began moving toward my locker. How could I trust him if he couldn't even show up to talk at lunch? Maybe I was on my own in all this.

When Mom picked me up at the end of the day, she acted as if nothing had happened that morning. She was her usual cheery self, rambling on about what she had done all day. Sometimes that was fine because I knew that I really didn't have to listen, just enough to nod at the right times. Other times, her over-the-top optimism grated on my very last nerve. Today was one of those days. Even though I didn't want have another fight, the sound of her voice was pushing me to lash out against it, to silence it. I wanted to yell, scream, shout. I wanted to tell her that her Pollyanna world did not exist—that the world was harsh and no one cared. I got my earbuds and put them in, hoping to block out her pointless prattle, hoping that she would get the message that I didn't feel like talking. Nope, not Mom. I don't even think she noticed that I'd put in my earbuds. As we pulled into our driveway, I turned my music off and heard Mom's surprised voice. "Isn't that the boy who helped us with the fall festival waiting by the front door?" My head spun in the direction of the door to see Kyle sitting patiently on our front stoop. What was he doing there? I didn't want to talk to him. I was mad at him for ditching me at lunch to hang out with Caleb.

"Mom, tell him he can't stay." My blunt words came out like searing bullets.

Instead, Mom—cheery, optimistic Mom—went over to Kyle and happily greeted him like a long-lost son. "Come in! We weren't expecting company, but I'm sure that Lacy will be glad to see you." She opened the door and ushered him into the kitchen "Make yourself at home. There are snacks in the fridge if you are hungry."

Kyle smiled and took a seat at the kitchen table. I glared at Mom and ran up to my room without talking to either of them. Dismayed at my behavior, I could hear Mom trying to smooth things over. "Oh, she's gone upstairs to change. She'll be down in a minute."

That's what she thought. I was *not* about to go downstairs to talk with anyone, least of all Kyle. I was ready to talk at lunch, and he wasn't there. I turned up my music, threw myself on my bed, and got out my diary. About five minutes later, there was a knock on my door. I knew that it had to be Mom. Still not wanting to talk, I began to sing as loudly as I could to block out the sound of her knocking. I stopped when I heard the stairs creaking. Hopefully now she would tell Kyle to leave. I waited a minute to listen to what was going on downstairs in the kitchen. I could hear voices mumbling but couldn't hear what was being said. I waited a bit longer, expecting the sound of a door closing as he left. There was more mumbling but no sound of anyone leaving. What were they talking about? I tiptoed out of my room to the top of the stairs to eavesdrop on the conversation. I strained to make sense out of the sounds, leaning out as far as I could over the railing without being seen.

"It would be easier to go down and join the conversation," came a voice from right next to me. Startled, I jumped, almost falling.

"Dad! You shouldn't sneak up on somebody like that!" I cried.

He nodded. "You know it's true though. Why don't you go down and talk to the boy?"

Vehemently, I shook my head from left to right.

"Why not?" he asked.

"He ditched me at lunch. He knew that I wanted to talk to him, and he didn't show up."

"He didn't show up?" questioned Dad, looking over the railing at Kyle. "Looks like he showed up to me."

"Well … I wanted to talk then."

"What's wrong with now?"

"That's not the point! He knew he was supposed to meet me at lunch, and he didn't. That's all there is to it."

"Is it? Did he say why he didn't talk to you at lunch?"

"At the very end, he mentioned Caleb as the bell was ringing."

"Aha!" exclaimed Dad. "So he did talk to you at lunch after all."

"No, not really. He got there a minute before the bell rang."

"So, did you find out *why* he didn't meet you?"

"Yeah, he said he was with Caleb," I answered, starting to feel exasperated.

"Wait a minute. You said he mentioned Caleb then the bell rang. Did you hear the rest of what he said?" asked Dad.

I didn't want to, but I had to admit that I hadn't. I was assuming he'd had lunch with Caleb.

"There you go. You don't have the full story. Stop jumping to conclusions, Lacy. Give the boy a chance."

I looked up. Dad was smiling at me hopefully, and although I still felt dissed by Kyle, I also felt that maybe Dad was right. Besides, Mom could be telling him anything, and I wouldn't know! I definitely didn't want her telling Kyle how much I liked him. As I made my way down the stairs, the voices were getting clearer. Whew! It sounded like the boring, run-of-the-mill stuff parents discussed with teenagers when they didn't know what else to say: school, sports, the weather. My foot was about to hit the last step when I heard "Mrs. Devlin, I think Lacy is in trouble. That's why I came here to talk to her." I stopped, frozen to the spot.

"Lacy, in trouble?" my mom's voice wavered.

"Oh! It's nothing horrible. She just said she wanted to talk. I guess she wants my help," continued Kyle, trying to sound like it wasn't a big deal.

"That's right," I interjected to their surprise. "I wanted to talk to Kyle at lunch, to get his opinion on something." I stared at Mom, hoping she'd catch on that I didn't want her there. Unfortunately, she continued to sit in the armchair, oblivious to my feelings.

"Lacy, it's so nice of you to join us." The terseness of her words cut into me, and I wanted to wound her as badly as her words hurt me. Knowing, however, that it would start WWIII and I'd never get to talk to Kyle, I took a deep breath and as calmly as I could asked her to leave the room. Obviously flustered and a bit insulted, Mom complied but not without reassuring us that she'd be around if we needed her.

With Mom out of the room, the awkwardness immediately set in. I had so much I wanted to say, but everything I thought of sounded lame. Kyle was sitting on the edge of his seat, waiting anxiously. Why did I do this to myself? I didn't even know if the words could physically come out. My mouth was so dry that I was sure they would stick in my throat. The pots and pans clanging and the beeping of the microwave told me that Mom was in the kitchen trying to listen in. Other than the noises emanating from the kitchen, the silence was deafening. Finally, neither of us could stand it any longer and spoke at the same time.

"Lacy …"

"Kyle …"

"No, you first."

"No, Lacy. Ladies first," he insisted.

I decided to get right to the point. "Kyle, why weren't you at lunch? You ate lunch with Caleb instead, didn't you?"

"Lacy, no. That's not what happened at all. Caleb and I had to make up a test, and it took longer than I thought."

Knowing that Kyle didn't intentionally ditch me was a relief. I felt foolish that I had doubted him.

"Oh, okay. Sorry. I'm just stressed over the whole thing with Faith."

"Oh ... yeah," agreed Kyle. "I wish there was something we could do to help her. I mean, we know that she didn't do it."

"Kyle, there is!" I exclaimed.

He looked at me blankly for a moment as my words registered. "Huh? What can *we* do?"

"I can prove that Faith didn't vandalize the restroom."

"Really? How? I don't understand."

I told him how I took pictures of the graffiti, but Kyle didn't see how that would help until I explained about the writing samples I had for the science fair project.

"That's awesome! So when are you going to talk to Pastor Dave about it?" he queried.

I was about to tell him that's why I wanted his advice when the doorbell rang. I ran to the front door to see who it could be. I was happily surprised to see Jade standing there on the other side of the door. Without so much as a hello, she breezed right into the living room "Oh, I see now why you haven't texted me back!" she said.

"Jade!" I hissed. "Be quiet. It's not what you think."

"Uh-huh," came her smug reply.

"Actually, I'm glad you're here. We're discussing what I texted you about last night."

"Oh, okay. I didn't know what you meant. I was falling asleep."

"No prob." So I explained again how I could prove that Faith was innocent so that Jade knew what was going on.

"Kyle thinks I should talk to Pastor Dave about it. What do you think, Jade?"

"Well, yeah. You're not just going to sit on info like that, are you?"

"No ... but ..." I started to reply.

Both of them stared at me like I was crazy and asked incredulously, "But what?"

"But ... but ... what if I say the wrong thing? What if he won't even talk to me? What if he doesn't believe me?"

"You have to have some self-confidence!" said Jade.

"But, Jade, why would anyone believe me when there are witnesses?"

"Witnesses?" she asked, looking puzzled.

"Yes, witnesses!" I cried adamantly. Then feeling like I needed corroboration, I turned to Kyle. "You know! You told me that there were people telling you that Faith vandalized the restroom and that I ratted her out."

Kyle nodded slowly in agreement.

"So, who was it, Kyle?" demanded Jade. "Tell us who started the rumor."

Put on the spot, Kyle was flustered and seemed annoyed at the question. Instead of giving us a straight answer, he looked away, mumbling that he had promised not to tell anyone.

"Seriously?" Jade practically spat the word at him. "Why not? You'd be able to help Faith!"

"Well … I promised," answered Kyle haltingly.

"You don't want Faith to be expelled, do you?" The harsh words flew out of my mouth before I could stop them.

"N … n … no. Of course not."

"So what's your problem?" asked Jade, sounding like she was interrogating a prisoner. "Tell us who it was!"

"But I don't want to get them in trouble. I mean, they trusted me," replied Kyle, obviously torn between helping one friend and possibly hurting another.

"Why would they get in trouble?" I asked naively.

"Lacy, they might be the ones who actually vandalized the school," explained Jade.

I hadn't exactly thought of that before, but hearing Jade say it, I could see the pieces of the puzzle falling into place. If they would spread false rumors, why wouldn't they be the ones who wrote the graffiti?

"What good would it do to know who told me anyway?" asked Kyle defensively. "Just because they said Faith did it doesn't mean that they did. I mean, someone else could've started the rumor."

We all thought a moment, pondering what to do.

"You have the photo and the writing samples, right?" Jade confirmed.

"Yup."

"So why not just bring those with you to talk to Pastor Dave?"

"Well, yeah. Of course," I replied, the exasperation evident in my voice. "But what if he brings up the witnesses who say that Faith did it?"

"Lacy, he must know who told Mrs. Strickland that it was Faith. He can question them if he likes."

I smiled then. "Jade, you're right! Why didn't I think of that?"

Realizing that we weren't going to insist that he tell us his sources, Kyle began to relax.

"Lacy, I do want to help. I'll go with you to talk to Pastor Dave if you want."

"Aw, thanks, Kyle. That'll be great! We'll talk to him tomorrow."

I met Kyle by the main doors first thing the next morning. We decided to talk to Pastor Dave as soon as possible. If we went before classes started, there'd be less of a chance that I would chicken out and change my mind. I wish I could say that we strode to his office full of confidence, but honestly, we were both super nervous. I kept smoothing my hair, and I noticed that Kyle was constantly clearing his throat. It was not that we were afraid of Pastor Dave—he was super nice and friendly—it was just, well, he was the *principal.* He had the power to believe or disbelieve what we were going to tell him. He also had the power to dole out punishments. I was praying that he would be granted God's wisdom in all of this and see that we were there to reveal the truth and not there to tattle. Hopefully he would recognize it as truth and rescind Faith's expulsion. Poor Faith. Nothing was worse than being convicted of a crime that you did not commit! We were almost to his office door when I could hear the reproachful voice of my mom playing in my head for the zillionth time. "Be careful. It's none of your business. Don't get involved. *You* don't want to get into trouble too." Why did she always tell me that? It was right to tell the truth and to stand up for your friends, wasn't it? I glanced at Kyle. What a sweetie! Here he was accompanying me even though he didn't have to. Even though it was hard, he was doing what was right. I put my shoulders back and my head high. *If he can do it, so can I! No matter how scared I am.* I knocked gently on the door and waited a couple of seconds. There was no response. Kyle and I looked at each other.

"Maybe he didn't hear you," offered Kyle. "Try again."

I knocked a bit louder and heard a muffled voice from behind the closed door. "Come in."

We slowly entered his office. I looked around to familiarize myself with the surroundings. This was where the troublemakers got sent to discuss their fate with Pastor Dave. I had never been in there before and had imagined it to be a dark and foreboding place, the curtains drawn, the room empty except for Pastor's Dave's desk, with a large Bible sitting on it and a straight high-back chair without a cushion for the accused directly facing the desk. In reality, the office was very homey and welcoming. The curtains were thrown open to allow the sun to shine in, illuminating the entire room. There was a small, round meeting table with comfortable chairs around it at one end of the room. At the other end, the wall was lined with books and photos of his family. Pastor Dave's polished mahogany desk stood in front of the bookshelf. There was a Bible on his desk that he was reading as well as other books and his laptop computer. To the side, he had his cup of coffee and doughnut. There were two large leather-looking chairs facing his desk. He motioned for us to take a seat. Although the atmosphere of the office put me more at ease, I was still reticent and didn't want to blurt out the story. Besides, I really didn't know where to begin, and I didn't want to mess up by saying something stupid.

"Good morning. I'll be with you in just a moment. I'm just finishing up a letter." Pastor Dave paused as he continued to type. "Voilà! All done." He smiled as he put away the computer and turned his full attention to us.

"What brings you two to see me this fine morning?"

I shifted in my seat, and Kyle cleared his throat, but neither of us said anything.

Pastor Dave leaned toward us. "You do want to talk with me, don't you?"

"Uh …" I started.

"Lacy has something to tell you," proffered Kyle.

I shot him a sarcastic look that said, "Yeah, thanks for your help," and shuffled the papers in my hand.

Pastor Dave prompted me again. "Is it about the papers you brought with you?"

I nodded yes and showed him the pictures I took of the graffiti.

"Why do you have these?" Pastor Dave asked with a grave tone.

"I was in the restroom and saw it, so I took a picture. Then Kate came in with Mrs. Strickland to show her while I was drying my hands."

"Uh huh. Who else was in the restroom?"

"No one. There was no one else in there when I got there," I replied flatly.

Pastor Dave sat back in his chair, rubbed his chin, then calmly asked, "So, why did you keep the photos, and why are you showing them to me now?"

"Well … I …" I stumbled over my words, not really knowing what to say next.

"The photos prove that it wasn't Faith who vandalized the school," interjected Kyle.

"How so?" queried Pastor Dave. "The vandal didn't sign her work, did she?" he asked with a smirk.

Knowing that my nerves had kicked in and I was tongue-tied, Kyle elbowed me in the ribs to jumpstart my brain.

"Ow, oh well, actually, sir, the vandal did sign her name in sort of a way." I explained then that my science fair project researched handedness and mentioned having the writing samples from the girls in my class.

Pastor Dave listened patiently for a few minutes and then stopped me. "Lacy, what does this have to do with the graffiti in the girls' restroom?"

I took a deep breath and dove right in. "My research proves that it couldn't have possibly been Faith who wrote those awful things."

Pastor Dave grimaced, shaking his head. "No, that has already been settled. Mrs. Strickland verified the writing, and there were witnesses."

I could feel my heart sink to the pit of my stomach. "But, Pastor Dave, I can prove it! Please take a minute and look at the samples."

He turned to check the time, then informed us that he only had a few minutes before he had to attend another meeting. I quickly took out the pictures and the samples to show him. He rifled through them, placing them on the desk in front of him. He had barely glanced at them when he stated firmly, hands on his hips, "Lacy, none of these are samples of Faith's handwriting. These don't prove anything. Now, I must be going to my meeting. Good day." With that statement, he ushered us out of his office and into the busy hallway. Kyle and I stood there staring at each other, stunned. The meeting had started out so well, and then … nothing.

Nothing had been accomplished. I didn't know what to say. I felt like a fool; my evidence wasn't any sort of proof according to Pastor Dave. The bell for class was about to ring, so, not wanting to get written up for being late, Kyle and I hurried to our classes, neither of us mentioning what had just happened. All class, I kept replaying the meeting with Pastor Dave in my mind. What had gone wrong? We told him our theory and showed him the evidence. That was all I had to do, wasn't it? The first chance I got, I texted Jade to tell her what happened.

"No way!" she exclaimed. "How could he not believe you?"

"IDK. I showed him the pictures and the writing samples from my science project."

"Why did he say that wasn't proof?"

"He said that Mrs. Strickland verified the handwriting and that there were witnesses." I wanted to wail and gnash my teeth, but no one could see that over a text. I'd been right; he was relying on witnesses, whoever they were.

Buzz. Buzz. I looked down to read Jade's reply, but to my surprise, the text was from Kyle.

"Been thinking. I have a sample of Faith's handwriting. We should go back to Pastor Dave and bring it with us."

That's right! That's why Pastor Dave had said I had no proof. I didn't have a sample of Faith's writing to compare to the graffiti. I hadn't included the letter she'd written to Kyle because he didn't know I had it. That would have been super awkward. If Kyle could produce a sample of her writing, there was still a chance! This had to work. The truth was at stake! Excitedly, I texted him back. "Great idea! TTYL," and immediately texted Jade the next part of our plan.

Kyle came in the next day with the note he had gotten from Faith. When he showed it to me, I did my best to hide that I had seen it before. It was the same note I had found in his notebook and photocopied.

"Kyle, this is great! It even points out how Faith was being bullied by the other girls."

"Yeah, I noticed that when I reread it. Get your other writing samples, and let's go talk to Pastor Dave."

I looked in my bag and searched my locker, but none of them were there. Befuddled, I turned to Kyle. "They aren't here!" I cried in anguish.

Kyle thought quickly. "That's okay. Pastor Dave has already seen them. It's the one in Faith's writing that he said he needs to see. We can find the other samples later."

We arrived at Pastor Dave's office as he was unlocking his door. "Good morning. What brings you two back to see me?"

"We have the proof you said you need," blurted Kyle. "We brought a sample of Faith's handwriting."

A shadow seemed to pass over Pastor Dave's face then, but he ushered us into his office anyway. "Well, I only have a few minutes, but since you have it with you, let's compare Faith's writing to the graffiti." Kyle passed the note over to Pastor Dave.

"Where's the picture of the graffiti that you had yesterday?" he queried. "We need that to compare the two styles of handwriting."

Kyle and I exchanged a worried glance. "Sir, we don't have it with us."

Immediately, Pastor Dave began to stand up from behind his desk, signaling that our meeting was over. "Well, without both of them, it is pointless to look at this now, so …"

"No!" my brain was screaming. "Don't let this happen. Don't let him dismiss the problem so easily. There must be a way to compare the two."

"So, you two go back to class and come see me when you find the photo," finished Pastor Dave.

That's it! The photo! I took a photo of the graffiti on my phone. I still had it on my phone.

"Wait!" I interjected loudly, startling both Kyle and Pastor Dave, who stopped short and stared at me inquisitively.

"I have the photo right here on my phone!" I exclaimed as I hurriedly searched through my bag for it. "Here it is!" I pulled it out triumphantly and found the picture to show Pastor Dave.

We all sat back down as Pastor Dave compared Faith's note to the picture. His demeanor quickly changed from one of aggravation at having his time wasted to one of incredulity. The difference between the two samples of handwriting was readily apparent. Everything about the two was different—the size and shape of the letters, the slant of the writing, even the pressure used by the writer while grasping the pen was obviously different. A look of concern came across Pastor Dave's face.

"It's too bad that you two didn't previously bring this to my attention. I will have to keep this note and investigate this matter further. Lacy, please print out a copy of this picture and give it to me. I prefer working with a hard copy." Then he handed me back my phone and gave us a pass to class.

Feeling jubilant and vindicated as we headed to our lockers, I gave Kyle a hug without thinking, exclaiming, "Thank you! We did it! We couldn't have done it without the note you brought in." I didn't realize what I had done until I saw his face turning a bright shade of pink and noticed that he was standing frozen like a stone statue, staring with a glazed over expression on his face. I quickly pulled away, rubbing my hands along my pants to give them something to do. "I … I … I only …" I stammered, feeling my face turn more crimson than his.

He gave me one of his amazing smiles, the kind that went from ear to ear, and agreed joyfully, "Yeah we did!" Then he took my hand and gave it a little squeeze before heading to his class. I had been afraid of what his reaction would be, but everything was going to be all right. In fact, I felt like it would be great. My hand was still tingling from his touch when I sat down in class. I wished that feeling would never go away!

I had to give Mrs. Strickland my pass from Pastor Dave since I was late for her class. She raised her eyebrows as she read where I had been, then curtly told me to take my seat. The science fair was right around the corner, so everyone had been given time to work with their partner in class on their project. Since Faith wasn't in school anymore, I had to work alone on the project. I took out the accordion file with my project in it. I had the research notes and my notebook, but the writing samples were missing. *Don't panic*, I kept telling myself over and over. *They have to be here somewhere.* Soon, I had everything that had been in my backpack out on my desk. The samples were nowhere to be found. Out of the corner of my eye, I could see Mrs. Strickland making her way over to my desk. *Oh no*, I thought. I didn't want to tell her that I didn't have my data with me. She would give me a zero for class participation for the day and might even write me up for being unprepared. Thankfully, the classroom phone buzzed, and I was spared. We all watched Mrs. Strickland, curious to know if one of us was getting dismissed or sent to the office. After saying yes and no numerous times, the only other thing she said was that she would be there in five minutes, after the end of this class period. Since the bell rang as she was hanging up the phone, I packed up all of my stuff without incident. Wondering who Mrs. Strickland had been talking with, I decided to follow her out of the classroom. I hoped that if I followed her, I could figure out who had phoned and possibly why. She was heading toward Pastor Dave's office! I watched her go in and close the door behind her. I waited a minute to see if I could hear what they were discussing, but with the door shut and the noise in the hallway, it was impossible.

Since I still had some time before the next class, I used the restroom across the hall. By the time I came out, the hallway was nearly empty. I was about to hurry to class when I heard raised voices. I looked up and down the hall, seeing nothing out of the ordinary. The voices softened and then sounded like yelling again. As I walked past Pastor Dave's office, I could hear Mrs. Strickland's high-pitched voice. "How dare you insinuate that I lied! I am a Christian just like you!" Part of me wished that I could stay and hear more, but my conscience was making me uncomfortable. I knew that eavesdropping was wrong.

I made my way to class, wondering what else was being said and what was going to happen. Mrs. Hart started the lesson only to be interrupted by the phone, "Okay, I'll send them down to your office," she stated before hanging up the receiver. She called Rachel and Aly up to her desk and handed them a pass. "Pastor Dave wants to see you in his office," she told them matter-of-factly. My mind was working overtime. Since we had Pastor Dave compare Faith's note and the graffiti side by side, he'd spoken with Mrs. Strickland and now Rachel and Aly. *They must be the ones who started the rumor about Faith*, I reasoned. Mrs. Hart continued the lesson, but all I kept thinking about was what was happening in Pastor Dave's office. I wished I could be a fly on the wall and know exactly what was happening without being noticed. Neither Alyssa nor Rachel returned before the end of class, and all I could do was imagine different scenarios of their meeting with Pastor Dave. Did they admit to bullying Faith? Did they admit to starting the rumor? Maybe it was one or both of them who actually wrote the graffiti. I really wanted to text Jade and Kyle to let them know what was going on. I hurriedly texted Jade between classes: "We did it! Operation Save Faith in motion."

Kyle and Caleb sat with me at lunch later, and it was almost like old times, except Faith wasn't there. Kyle had filled Caleb in on my plan to prove Faith's innocence. Caleb apologized for how mean he had been and asked if I could forgive him for believing that I could have betrayed his sister, which of course I did. I mean, I knew that the whole mess had been stressful for all of us. Caleb thanked us for talking with Pastor Dave and said he would let Faith know what truly good friends we were. Then he asked if we knew who actually wrote the graffiti. Both Kyle and I shook our heads no.

"Well … not exactly, but we narrowed it down, we think," I added.

"How's that?" Caleb wanted to know.

"Apparently, the person who did it is a lefty, given the slant of the handwriting," I answered.

"Oh … hey, did you check the handwriting on the note that Faith got in her locker?" he asked after a moment of thought. "Is it the same writing as in the bathroom?"

They both waited anxiously for my answer. "Yes, I did. And no, it didn't. The handwriting isn't at all the same. Actually, it looks like a righty wrote the note."

We sat in silence for a few moments, and then Caleb asked, "Do you have them with you? Can I look at them to compare them?"

Why not? I thought and reached for my bag. I might not have had the writing samples for my project, but I did still have the note Caleb gave me, and I had the picture of the graffiti on my phone. Caleb analyzed them and agreed that they didn't look like the same person had written them, and he confirmed that the graffiti looked nothing at all like Faith's writing. Leaning closer to them, I whispered my suspicion that Alyssa and Rachel were probably the culprits. Seeing the slightly surprised expressions on their faces, I explained that Alyssa was a lefty, Rachel was a righty, and they both liked to write in black marker.

"Did Faith tell you how she defended me in English class against them?" I asked. "And how they hid her lunch from her one day?"

"No, she didn't. She didn't really tell me too much of what happened," Caleb answered, gritting his teeth.

Suddenly I remembered that I hadn't seen either of them for a while. I looked to see if they were at their usual lunch table, only to see two empty spots where they generally sat. When I told Kyle and Caleb how first Mrs. Strickland and then Alyssa and Rachel had been called to the office, they raised their eyebrows, and Kyle gave a long, low whistle. Caleb then thanked us again for showing everything to Pastor Dave and for restoring his faith in humanity.

I left lunch beaming. It felt wonderful to tell the truth and to help a friend. My joy was cut short, however, by the ringing of the telephone in my next class. I was instructed to go to Pastor Dave's office immediately. Suddenly nervous, I glanced around the room to see if Alyssa and Rachel had returned yet. They still weren't back. *Oh great*, I couldn't help but think. *I'm going to have to defend myself and Faith in front of them by myself!* This was not going to be fun. Alyssa and Rachel were going to back each other up, no matter what. Who did I have to help me make my case? I rounded the corner, almost to Pastor Dave's office, when I heard footsteps behind me. I peeked over my shoulder to see Kyle strolling up behind me.

He smiled. "I guess this is it," he commented.

"What's it?" I asked, not understanding.

"You know, it's going down. The big meeting to clear Faith. Did you print out the graffiti picture?" he asked confidently.

"Oh no! I haven't had time to do that. Please tell Pastor Dave that I went to the library to print it out!" I exclaimed as I changed course toward the library.

"Okay, but hurry!" Kyle said as he reached the office door.

I raced into the library with my phone, hoping that Ms. Martin could help me print the picture. Fortunately, she was sitting at the front desk. "Sure. What do you need?" she asked cheerily. Two minutes later, I had the picture printed in my hand.

"Thanks!" I called as I hurried to Pastor Dave's office. Adrenaline pumping, hands shaking, and my stomach in knots, I arrived in front of the office door. I knew that I should go in, but I was so nervous! To calm myself, I stopped for a moment to pray. "Dear Lord, thank you for always being there. Please be with me now. Help me to bring the truth out in the light. Amen." I felt a sense of peace and calm wash over me as I knocked on the door and proceeded to enter.

The office was packed with people. Mrs. Strickland, Alyssa, and Rachel were sitting at the conference table. Pastor Dave and Kyle were standing by his desk. To my surprise, Faith was even there sitting in one of the comfy chairs in front of the desk. She smiled a genuine smile and waved when I walked in the door.

"Good. Let's all take a seat at the conference table," instructed Pastor Dave. After all of us had taken a seat, he started out saying, "This meeting has been convened to promote justice and truth. Let us pray that the Lord works mightily in our hearts so that the truth in all things be revealed, for our God is a just and holy God. Amen.

"I asked you all here today so that we may get to the bottom of how the graffiti came to be written in the girls' restroom. As you know, new information has come to my attention, and I feel that the best way to address the situation is to have us all discuss it together. Before yesterday, I hadn't personally seen the graffiti in question but had relied solely on eyewitness accounts. Now, after having seen it and compared it to the accused's handwriting, there are serious doubts in my mind as to who the real perpetrator was." Pastor Dave paused a moment, taking in the expressions of everyone at the table. By far, the happiest person there was Faith, who hadn't really smiled for weeks. Pastor Dave turned to address me. "Lacy, were you able to bring a printout of the picture?" he asked.

"Yes," I answered as I handed it across the table to him.

"As you can all see," continued Pastor Dave as he pulled out the sample note that Kyle had given him yesterday, "the handwriting in these two examples is quite different." Then he passed them around for all of us to compare the handwriting. Kyle and Faith passed the samples down to Mrs. Strickland, who inspected them quite closely, as if trying to prove Pastor Dave wrong. Not finding any similarity to point out, she handed them to Alyssa and Rachel, who were still playing the part of innocent bystanders, not wanting any blame to fall on them. They read the note and scowled at Faith, grumbling something about not being mean.

"Ladies, if you have something to say, please address the whole group. Do you have something to add to the discussion?" asked Pastor Dave calmly.

As they were shaking their head no, Mrs. Strickland asked for someone to pass the water down to her. Rachel quickly grabbed the pitcher of water, bumping my hand as I reached for the papers. Rachel dropped the pitcher on the table, water spilling everywhere and ruining the papers in the process. Shocked by the turn of events, I sat there holding the sopping wet papers as they disintegrated in my hand. Faith's face fell when she saw what happened. Kyle and I stared unbelievingly at what used to be the proof of Faith's innocence. Rachel apologized but did not lift a finger to help mop up the mess. Mrs. Strickland, seeming to smirk, used the few napkins that were on the table to sop up the water and instructed Alyssa to get some paper towels. The only person in the room who wasn't flustered was Pastor Dave. After it was all cleaned up, Pastor Dave continued as if nothing had happened. "After having seen both samples, I'm sure you agree that it wasn't the same person who wrote both."

Mrs. Strickland shook her head in disagreement. "No, it is impossible to tell because two different type of writing instruments were used; one was written in pen, and the other in thick marker. That would affect how the handwriting looks."

Rachel and Alyssa agreed with Mrs. Strickland's assessment.

"Actually," I said, "the research I've done for my science project shows that the pen or pencil used doesn't affect the basic style of someone's writing. If there is a slant to their writing, there will always be a slant. If they connect their t's and h's, they will always be connected."

"So, the fundamentals of someone's handwriting doesn't change because of the writing instrument. Interesting," said Pastor Dave. "But if we wanted to test this to find out if it is true or not, what would we do?"

We all looked uncomfortably around the table from one to another, waiting for someone else to answer. Time dragged on until Faith spoke up. "I could write something with a marker like the vandal used."

"Faith, that is a fine idea," said Pastor Dave. "Let's see. Here is a piece of paper. Now we just need a marker." Pastor Dave got up and rummaged through his desk for a couple of moments. "Does anyone have a black marker?" he asked casually.

"Oh, I have one," answered Rachel and took out her thin black marker.

Mrs. Strickland looked over at the marker. "Oh, no, the graffiti was written in thick marker, I believe."

Rachel nudged Alyssa. "You must have one with you. You use those all the time."

Alyssa shot her a look as if to say, "Shut up! Why did you say that?" but she opened her purse and pulled out a chunky black marker.

"Perfect," commented Pastor Dave. "Faith, please write a couple of sentences so that we can see your handwriting when using the marker."

Unsure of herself, Faith asked *what* she should write. Pastor Dave shrugged and told her that it didn't really matter what she wrote, that what mattered was her handwriting.

Hearing this, Mrs. Strickland disagreed. "Shouldn't she write what the vandal wrote so that we can compare the writing?"

Rachel agreed that it wouldn't make any sense to check her handwriting if we couldn't directly compare it to the graffiti.

At a loss, Faith whimpered, "But we don't have the picture of the graffiti anymore. I don't know what it said."

Then Alyssa added, "So why bother? The picture is gone, so there's nothing to compare her handwriting to anyway."

At that statement, Faith looked around the table, distraught at the thought that her name would not be cleared. "Then how can I prove that I wasn't the one who did it?" mumbled Faith.

Kyle elbowed me to get my attention. What did he want? Clearly, things weren't working out the way they were supposed to. I could feel Faith's tension and sadness, and combined with my own, a feeling of despondency was setting in. I couldn't help but feel that it was a lost cause. Kyle nudged me again, and I saw him mouth the words "Your phone." What about my phone? What did he mean? No one had called me. I had turned it off at the beginning of the meeting.

While I was trying to figure out what he was talking about, I could hear Pastor Dave as if he was far off in another dimension "Well, if there are no suggestions …"

No suggestions? What did he mean? Was the meeting over?

Kyle kicked my shins. "Ow!" Everyone turned to look in my direction. "I … I … my phone," I babbled.

"Your phone?" repeated Pastor Dave.

And suddenly I understood. "My phone. I have the picture of the graffiti on my phone. I can go print out another copy."

A smile spread across Pastor Dave's face. "Of course! Yes, Lacy, please go print out another copy. We'll wait until you return."

I sprinted out of the office toward the library. Thankfully, Ms. Martin was available to help. In fact, she printed off five extra copies. "Just in case," as she said.

When I got back, Rachel, Alyssa, and Mrs. Strickland had left to use the restroom. Since we had a couple of minutes, Faith and I also went to the restroom. As we entered, we could hear snippets of their conversation.

"How did Lacy get the picture of the graffiti?" asked Rachel.

"I bet she's the one who actually wrote it!" declared Alyssa. "How else would she have it? We weren't allowed in the restroom after it was found."

Horrified at the accusation, I hid in the stall until they all left. Were they going to accuse me of being the vandal now? My stress now doubled, and my stomach lurched. "Please God," I prayed, "please don't let the unjust win."

When everyone returned to the office, the meeting reconvened. Pastor Dave gave a picture of the graffiti and the marker to Faith and asked her to copy it in her own handwriting. A minute later, Pastor Dave was holding the two up, comparing them as we watched. It was evident that the handwriting was not at all similar. Pastor Dave looked at Faith kindly and asked her to forgive him and the staff for the terrible mistake. He also indicated that he would call her parents to apologize and to formally invite Faith back to the school. Faith beamed and heaved a huge sigh of relief that her ordeal was over. I leaned over and gave Faith a congratulatory hug. Mrs. Strickland offered Faith neither apology nor congratulations but sat scowling in her seat, obviously angered at having been outed as a liar. She had immediately accused Faith of being the culprit without taking the time to look at the style of handwriting. She hadn't even compared it to Faith's writing, which would have been easy considering all of the homework and classwork that we did for her. Instead, she had chosen to accept without question what witnesses told her. It appeared that she had wanted to believe that Faith committed the crime. By her demeanor, it seemed that our happiness actually aggravated Mrs. Strickland.

Our joy was soon dashed though as questions as to who the actual vandal was were brought forth. Mrs. Strickland bitterly posed the question,

"Well, if it wasn't Faith, who was it? We still have to catch the student who did this."

Rachel then asked smugly, "Lacy, how did you get the pictures of the graffiti? The restroom was closed as soon as it was noticed."

All eyes were on me then. "I was in the bathroom after class, and I saw it," I explained.

Rachel continued, "Oh, I was just wondering because it wasn't there in the morning before school. All of us were in there fixing our hair. We would have seen it."

Alyssa chimed in, "Yeah, we would have. Hey, how do we know that it wasn't Lacy? She was one of the last people in there before it was reported."

Faith turned to me with wide eyes and squeezed my hand for support. Pastor Dave turned to me. "Lacy, would you mind writing the graffiti with the marker?" Upset and insulted at being accused, I picked up the marker and gave him a sample of my writing, knowing that it would look nothing like the true culprit's handwriting. A moment later, I was vindicated as Pastor Dave pointed out how different my writing was from the original graffiti.

Kyle smirked. "Of course it wasn't Faith or Lacy. They are both righties."

I nodded. "Kyle is right. The graffiti was definitely written by someone left-handed, as you can see from the slant of the lettering. When I was working on my science project, I thought it was interesting that there are only a few lefties in my class, Alyssa, Kate, and Aimee."

As I finished my sentence, all eyes turned to Alyssa. "What?" she cried. "You think I … just because I'm a lefty!"

"Alyssa, why don't *you* give us a writing sample? You can use your *own* black marker," challenged Kyle as he pushed the paper and marker toward her.

Hesitantly, Alyssa picked up the marker and copied the graffiti. Pastor Dave took the sample to examine. Holding it up to compare it to the original, he conceded that the slant of the words was similar, showing that the culprit was indeed left-handed. Alyssa nervously squirmed in her seat and began playing with her hair while Pastor Dave continued to analyze her handwriting. "However, the formation of the letters is quite different," added Pastor Dave. "No, Alyssa isn't the vandal either."

Upset at having been wrongly accused and feeling that it was unfair, Alyssa turned to Rachel. "Rachel, you may as well write a sample too. All of us had to," she stated emphatically.

"Fine then," retorted Rachel, who never backed away from a challenge. She grabbed the paper and began to write the sample but was having trouble using the chunky marker. "Sorry, I can't write with that one. I'll use mine," she said as she pulled out her calligraphy pen. Pastor Dave compared her sample to the graffiti, just as he had done with the others. It was clear to everyone that the handwriting wasn't the same, especially since Rachel was a righty. I had to keep myself from audibly gasping though; the sample looked exactly like the handwriting of the mean note Faith had gotten in her locker. I would have to show it to Pastor Dave before the end of the day.

"So, now what do we do?" wondered Alyssa. "Should we have all the left-handed girls write a sample?"

Instead of answering her question, Pastor Dave turned to Mrs. Strickland. "Mrs. Strickland, tell us again how you became aware of the vandalism."

Mrs. Strickland sat up straighter and cleared her throat before beginning. "I was preparing for class when Kate ran into the room saying that there was a problem in the girls' restroom. I quickly followed her, expecting that one of the students had become ill. In fact, when I first arrived on the scene, Lacy was drying her hands, and I asked her if she was all right, thinking maybe she had been sick. She informed me that she was fine, and Kate called me over to the stall where the graffiti was written. Upon seeing it, I came straight here to your office," Mrs. Strickland finished with a look of self-importance.

"So, Kate came to tell you about the graffiti?" verified Pastor Dave.

"Yes, yes, that's right. It was Kate who let me know about it," answered Mrs. Strickland confidently.

At that, Pastor Dave picked up the phone on his desk. We heard him say, "Please send Kate Houghton down to my office immediately."

Moments later, there was a timid knock at the door. Kate came in slowly, her eyes growing wide when she saw all of us sitting around the table. "Kate please take a seat," instructed Pastor Dave as he pulled the chair to his desk over to the table. "I asked you to come so that you could tell us what you know about the graffiti in the girls' restroom."

Kate stared blankly for a minute, then repeated what he'd said in a questioning tone, "Graffiti? In the restroom?" No one said anything. Then Kate looked at Faith and added, "Oh, do you mean what she wrote a couple of weeks ago?"

Faith started to look angry, like she was ready to yell at Kate. Thankfully though, she noticed me shaking my head no and thought better of it. Pastor Dave noticed Faith's reaction as he responded calmly to Kate, "Yes, that's the graffiti I mean. Kate, can you remember what happened that day? Please share with us all that you remember."

"Well, I had gone into the restroom between classes, like I always do. While I was in there, I noticed the writing all over the stall I was using. It was awful and mean what was written there. So I went and got a teacher right away to show them what had happened."

"Kate, do you remember which teacher you told?" asked Pastor Dave.

"It was Mrs. Strickland. You remember—right, Mrs. Strickland?"

Mrs. Strickland nodded her agreement.

"Kate, do you remember seeing anyone else in the restroom around the time you were there?" questioned Pastor Dave.

Kate thought a moment. "No ... no one else was there," stated Kate, thinking out loud. "Wait ... wait ... Lacy, you were there, weren't you?" said Kate.

I nodded. "Yeah, you ran past me out the door when I was going in."

"Yeah, that's right," said Kate. "And you were drying your hands when I got back with Mrs. Strickland."

"Kate, you're remembering a lot. That's very helpful," said Pastor Dave. "How did you know that Faith was the person who wrote the graffiti?"

Kate looked thoughtful and paused a moment. "I don't know."

Pastor Dave then asked, "Did you tell Mrs. Strickland that that was Faith's handwriting?"

"No, no. I don't know what her handwriting looks like."

"So, after you showed it to Mrs. Strickland, what happened next?" queried Pastor Dave.

"She stormed out of the restroom," answered Kate.

"When she left, what did *you* do?" questioned Pastor Dave.

"I don't know. It all happened so fast."

"What happened so fast?" asked Pastor Dave, trying to keep an even tone.

"Well, everybody came to ask me what was going on. They wanted to know why Mrs. Strickland was so upset."

"And did you tell them?"

"Yeah, I told them that someone wrote awful, mean things in the bathroom. They wanted to know what it said, so I told them."

"Was that all?" Pastor Dave wanted to know.

"Well, they asked me if I knew who did it, and I said I didn't know. Then everyone tried to guess who might have done it."

"Was Mrs. Strickland there when the students were discussing who did it?"

"Well, sort of," replied Kate. "She saw everybody in little groups talking loudly about it and made us stop, clear the hallway, and go to class."

"I see," said Pastor Dave. "Kate, while you're here, we'd appreciate it if you would help us with an experiment. All of the girls here have written out what the graffiti said in their own handwriting. We'd like you to do the same. Here is a picture of the graffiti for you to copy," explained Pastor Dave as he set the picture, some paper, and the thick black marker in front of her.

Kate balked; it was obvious that she did not want to copy the graffiti. She turned in Alyssa and Rachel's direction with a pleading look. "But... but," she stammered. "Why? You already know that *she* did it," Kate said, pointing the marker at Faith.

Rachel and Alyssa began examining their nails, not wanting to look at Kate.

"Kate, new evidence has been brought to my attention, and it is unclear who actually wrote the graffiti," explained Pastor Dave. "Please just copy what is in the photograph."

"Oh, I remember now who said it was Faith," blurted Kate. "I overheard Rachel and Alyssa talking right before Mrs. Strickland made us go to class. They said it was Faith. They said that she was fake, that she wasn't really nice at all. They said that Faith had said mean things about them in English class."

Kate's diversion worked. Pastor Dave turned his attention to Alyssa and Rachel. "Why didn't the two of you mention this before?"

Rachel sheepishly answered, "It didn't seem important."

Faith was becoming angrier by the minute. She sat glaring at the girls, grinding her teeth. I wanted to tell her that it would be okay, but how could I in the middle of the meeting?

Pastor Dave turned back to Kate, stating sternly, "Kate, I'm instructing you to copy the picture of the graffiti now."

Kate, not thinking of any way out of the situation, picked up the marker and scrawled the words that had been written in the bathroom stall. She handed it to Pastor Dave, her eyes brimming with unshed tears. Pastor Dave held the two papers side by side. The similarity was amazing. Kate's sample was almost an exact match; it was almost as if she had traced it! Before Pastor Dave could say anything, Kate was pointing at Rachel and Alyssa, exclaiming as she wiped the tears from her face, "They told me to do it! It was their idea. They wanted to get back at Faith. I didn't want to do it. It was all their idea!"

Rachel and Alyssa stared at Kate with a horrified expression and began shaking their heads vigorously in disagreement. Soon they were yelling at one another, each one accusing their friend of wrong doing. The situation had escalated rapidly, and Pastor Dave had to physically separate the girls, who had started shoving one another, and order them to sit back down and be quiet. After restoring order, Pastor Dave turned to Kyle, Faith, and me. "Thank you for coming to talk to me. You all have been very helpful and patient. You can go back to class now. Faith, I will call your family and inform your teachers that you will be returning tomorrow."

Faith and Kyle nodded and left, but I hung back. "Pastor Dave, can I talk with you one more minute?"

"Sure," he answered as he walked me to the hallway.

I pulled the copy of the note that had been left in Faith's locker out of my purse. "I think that you should see this too. I forgot about it until I saw Rachel's writing sample," I said as I handed it to him.

Upon seeing it, he immediately understood. "Thank you. I just wish that you kids had shown me these earlier." I nodded solemnly and went to the last class of the day.

The rest of the year was a happy blur. Of course Faith came back to school, and we became practically inseparable. We worked on our handedness project almost nonstop up until the day of the science fair. The project was a lot of fun, and we were even going to set up a handwriting booth at the fair where people could have their handwriting analyzed. I enjoyed researching the info and analyzing the data. However, I wasn't thrilled about making a poster board or slideshow to present on the day of the fair. Thankfully, Faith was back, so I could leave that up to her. She was definitely more artsy than I was and better at creating presentations on the computer.

Before I knew it, the day of the science fair had arrived. All students had to bring in their project and presentation by eight o'clock Wednesday morning so that the judges could read all of the papers, interview us, the scientists, and decide on a winner by 8:00 p.m. However, the relief I felt at having finished the project wasn't complete because the interview part of the competition, which I was dreading, was imminent. Who decided that we had to speak with the judges and answer their questions? Speaking to, well, anyone was definitely not my strength. I would have to explain the project, our hypotheses, data collection and analysis, and how the scientific method worked in our project. Faith knew how nervous I got, so we took turns role-playing the presentation. She was so cool! She made it fun by asking me questions in a foreign accent. I think she was trying to sound Russian, but she sounded more British to me. We were practicing our presentation one last time as everyone began filtering into the multipurpose room for the event. I was about to explain the hypothesis when I felt someone rush up behind me, but when I turned around to see who it was, no one was there. I turned back to look at Faith and saw an amused smirk on her face.

"Did you see someone just a minute ago?" I asked her.

"*Nyet*. Finish answering the question," she responded in her ridiculous fake accent, trying not to laugh.

I went to answer but then felt a bit of warm air on my neck, close to my ear. I whirled around, determined to catch the culprit. To my bewilderment, there was still no one there, just a group of middle schoolers chatting with their friends.

"You must have seen who it was this time!"

Faith shook her head no, but her eyes were laughing at me from behind her thick eyelashes.

She asked me the question again. This time, I was halfway through the answer when I spotted Jade peeking out from behind Faith's shoulder.

"Jade! You're here!" I cried, running over to give her a hug. "You could've just said hello instead sneaking up on me."

"Of course I came to cheer on you and Faith," said Jade, smiling, "but I only just got here. What are you talking about?"

"You mean it wasn't you behind me?"

Then I heard muffled laughter and saw a streak of blond hair move behind the stack of chairs near us.

"Kyle? Kyle, I see you!" I called out.

Kyle popped out from behind the chairs, laughing.

"I couldn't help myself," he said with a twinkle in his eye.

Everyone was circulating within the multipurpose room now, observing the science projects and talking to the students about them. The judges were also making their way around the tables, conducting the final interviews. Fortunately, Faith and I were one of the first ones interviewed. The judge, Mr. Nunes, smiled kindly and asked us three or four questions. Amazingly, I wasn't nervous and easily answered the questions. It was weird! I didn't even have to think about the answers; they just rolled right off of my tongue. Faith even said that I sounded confident.

Faith and I took turns manning our handwriting station and walking around checking out the other exhibits. Of course there were exhibits on the formation of crystals, the durability of different brands of nail polish, and which type of wrapper kept food fresher longer. Kyle joined me as soon as his interview was over.

"So, which one do you like best?" he asked.

"Hmmm. My favorite is Hailey's."

"Oh, you only like it because she brought in cute little chicks," Kyle chided.

"So! They're adorable!"

"Have you seen the one about distracted driving?"

I shook my head no.

"You have to see it," he answered, grabbing my hand and pulling me in that direction. "It's so cool! There's even a video."

The warmth of Kyle's hand holding mine made me feel all warm and tingly too. This was turning out to be a great evening.

Soon, though, it was almost over. The judges had interviewed everyone and tallied the results of the competition. Pastor Dave asked the audience to take their seats as the winners of the science fair were announced. A hush fell over the room as we awaited the results.

"As judges, we would like to thank all of the students for sharing their interesting projects here tonight. It is evident that a lot of hard work went into them. Believe me when I say that it was a challenge for us to pick only three winners."

Kyle leaned over to whisper in my ear, "You'll probably win. Your project is awesome!"

I didn't think so, but I still liked the compliment. Before I got a chance to answer, the judges began announcing the winners.

"Third place, for their project on the circulatory system—Timothy Reed and Michael Mills. Please come to the front to receive your award."

Everyone applauded as Tim and Mike accepted their yellow ribbon.

"Second place goes to Rachel Buttrick and Alyssa Montoya for their work on nail polish durability."

We clapped politely as Rachel and Alyssa sashayed up to the front to collect their prize. I glanced over at Faith to see her reaction. Even though Faith said she forgave Rachel and Alyssa for bullying her, I knew there was still some tension between them. They were definitely not all friends. Although Faith was clapping, her grimace gave away her true feelings.

Kyle squeezed my hand as the judge began, "The project that won first place isn't the typical science fair project. It is intriguing and clearly interesting to people of all ages, as evidenced by the number of visitors to the exhibit this evening."

I looked over at Kyle, mouthing the words, "No way."

At about the same time, Faith elbowed me and said, "Nope, not us."

Suddenly I felt Kyle squeezing my hand more tightly as he shouted over the applause, "I was right! You won!"

What? Then I heard the judge call our names again.

"Lacy Devlin and Faith Barrett, please come up to receive your award."

I could hardly believe it, and from the surprised look on Faith's face, I could tell that she felt the same way.

Kyle gently shoved us toward the podium, since we were practically paralyzed with disbelief.

When I got up to the front, I could see everyone clapping, especially Mom, who was also cheering. Caleb caught our attention and gave us a huge thumbs-up.

Then it was over. Pastor Dave thanked the students for all of their hard work and everyone for attending the science fair. The science teachers instructed us to take our project on the way out.

Mom was so proud she had us stop to take pictures with our ribbon in front of our exhibit. Kyle helped us dismantle our exhibit and collect the poster board and handwriting station materials. Then we headed to Mom's car. After everything was in the trunk and we had said bye to Faith, the most amazing thing happened. Kyle nervously took my hand and turned to face me.

"Lacy… um… Lacy, the spring banquet is in a few weeks, and …"

Kyle's palms were sweaty, but I didn't care! All I could do was stare up at him with a gigantic, goofy grin on my face.

"Well, I was wondering … I mean …"

"Oh, I heard that the banquet is a lot of fun."

"Yeah," he said, starting to smile, "and, hey, maybe you could wear that dress I saw you in when I first visited your house?"

"Kyle! Are you inviting me to the banquet?" I asked teasingly.

"Yeah, I guess I am," he answered shyly, shuffling his feet.

"Yes! I'd love to!" I exclaimed.

"Best night ever!" That would be my next text to Jade.

You, Lord, are forgiving and good, abounding
in love to all who call to you.
—Psalm 86:5 NIV

Bibliography

Holy Bible, New King James Version. Thomas Nelson, 1982.

Lee, Harper. *To Kill a Mockingbird*. J.B. Lippincott & Co., 1960.

Redman, Matt. *10,000 Reasons*, Spirit & Song: Disc M, 2013.

About the Author

Felicity T. Abbott is a veteran Christian teacher who enjoys working with pre-teens and teenagers. She often mentors students as they deal with life's experiences and helps students gain a Christian perspective on life and everyday difficulties. This is her first book.

CPSIA information can be obtained
at www.ICGtesting.com
Printed in the USA
BVHW030754020321
601488BV00012B/38

9 781664 212527